BEGINNING

Dylan Alexander

BEGINNING

DAWN

And here is where all begins and ends.

Brian McDaniel's fingers tapped along the table. He was waiting impatiently alongside his colleague, Colonel Leslie Thompson, for Daniel Lockhart, the Chairman of the powerful military and science company, New Horizons. In Brian's line of work as a clinical cytologist, he never had to wait very long for anyone to meet with him. Leslie, however, was happy to have at least a little downtime. Finally, Daniel entered the room. He nodded at the others as he sat at the table.

"Sorry I'm late," Daniel began. "I was seeing Amy and Marcus off. They've just hit the beds. I plan to do the same shortly."

"I was about to do so myself," said Brian. Daniel looked regretfully at the man and told him, "I'm afraid that won't be possible."

Brian frowned.

"Why is that?" he asked. Daniel averted his eyes. It was hard to ask such a thing of two people who had been so good to him, especially after what had happened.

"I need you to stay here, up top, with Leslie," he finally said, taking many a pause to find the correct words. "I need you both to do me a favor."

"And what might that be?" Leslie asked, now very interested in what Daniel had to say. Again, he took his time thinking of the right way to explain it.

"When we arrive at Eden," he started, "I want us to rebuild as an ideal society. Leslie, you said this ship contains records of all the most important events in human history leading up to what happened. I need you and Brian, over the course of our voyage, to examine these records thoroughly. I need you to look at every successful action humanity has ever taken in its path of evolution and compose a strategic document out of them. This document will tell us what we need to do to create an everlasting utopia."

The air in the room was heavy, but all three of those present were certain this was the right thing to do.

"Also, I'd like you to focus primarily on human rights and their development," Daniel proceeded. "I believe this new society should be founded on those rights, and that they should be respected far better by our new humanity, as it is indeed possible that Man's disregard for them helped precipitate what happened, along with Brian's theory, of course."

Brian recalled the interview, feeling knowledgeable and remorseful simultaneously.

"And as for the theory," Daniel added, looking straight at the cytologist, "see to it nothing like that *ever* happens again. I'm not sure how you can manage it, but if you can—."

"Every measure will be taken," Leslie interjected, now also facing Brian. Guilt and pride clashed within the scientist: pride in the fact that he was the man for the job, guilt in the fact that...

The officer and Brian were, though still composed, astounded by what was being asked of them. They realized the responsibility this man was placing on the two of them and, regardless of any reluctant thoughts, they had to accept it. This was what their journey was all about. Humanity needed to succeed from now on. If it failed again—it couldn't fail again.

"Do you both understand?" Daniel asked. His eyes were hard and direct. The two nodded in agreement, slowly.

"We'll do whatever it takes, sir," Leslie said. Daniel clenched his teeth behind closed lips, then said, "Good. That is all."

He left the others alone to ponder how they would go about their mission. Brian kept shaking his head, pictures of all that had brought them to that fateful moment racing through his mind: pain, destruction, defeat, betrayal, sorrow, utter annihilation. It all left him with just one question, one for which he had no valid answer, no solid truth:

"How did we come to this?"

BOARDING

Daniel Lockhart watched with relief as his wife, Amy, and young son, Marcus, crossed the elevated boarding platform into the *Guardian*. The boy beamed at the giant spacecraft as he entered it. His father beamed too, but not at the ship. The child had finally awoken, and it had been found that his memory was at least somewhat intact. There was also confirmation that Marcus' prior aggression would no longer be in control of him, confirmation provided by Brian. This lifted an even greater deal of weight from Daniel's shoulders.

Before boarding himself, he stood in awe, absorbing the immensity of the silo they were within one last time. Then, turning to his friend, Leslie, he asked her, "Are there any historical records aboard the *Guardian* I don't know about yet?"

"Every major event in human history," Leslie began, "is aboard it, save the most recent one, of course."

"Is that so?" said Daniel, a plan formulating in his mind. "You said it would take twenty to thirty years for us to get to Eden. Are the stasis beds that were scheduled to be installed finished?"

"Indeed," Leslie answered, wondering what Daniel was designing in that head of his. Her curiosity subsided quickly. She was thinking of someone. Her eyes wavered as the thought rolled through her mind. There it was, in the water, slowly descending to the ocean floor. She shook the image off.

About three hours of boarding passed as crowds crossed the massive gangplank and entered the *Guardian*. Everyone had to be within the ship's many passenger levels and safely buckled into their seats prior to departure. After the estimated fourteen hundred and fifty people (crew included) were safely aboard, the enormous ship tilted vertically until its nose faced directly upward. The flight crew, led by Leslie, was bustling, activating all of the ship's primary systems. Leslie had previously led the flight crew of the *Vanguard,* a ship used for planetary exploration.

In her chair on the bridge, she was solemn, glancing over the flight deck and contemplating the all too short passenger list. In a perfect world, the entire population of Earth would be loaded onto the vessel. But, as attested by preceding crises, imperfection was the order of the day. Saving these few for the sake of the species was the best that could be done, given the circumstances.

Though Eden was a good distance off, at least it was there. At least there was something. They would soon be taking off. They would soon leave the dying planet.

CHILDREN

Kenro was tired. He couldn't sleep. Although everything was going according to plan, he couldn't shut his eyes for too long. He didn't know why. Perhaps it all seemed too easy, after what had happened. It did feel a bit like a dream, or, more accurately, a nightmare.

"I like the quiet," the man next to him whispered. Kenro turned to look upon the serene face of the Dalai Lama. His eyes were closed and his head was tilted back against the seat.

"It makes for a nice ride," he went on. Kenro envied him. Even after the horrors of recent memory, the Dalai Lama still managed to rest. No one else on the transport could do the same. Through the dim light, Kenro could see their faces. They were like him, wide awake. They weren't talking, just looking, hearing, feeling. It all seemed too good to be true, and yet, in actuality, it *wasn't* too good to be true at all. It made sense for this to be the way out. It made sense for them to survive, to live on.

"What do you think, Mr. Chauren? Is it too dark in here?"

Kenro kept eyeing the faces as he said, "I'd rather it were brighter."

"Sometimes the darkness helps," the Dalai Lama told him. "It can be calming."

"What if I don't want to be calm?"

"Oh? And why wouldn't you want that?"

Kenro sighed. He knew his answer wouldn't prove satisfactory.

"I just don't like the idleness is all," he said, and the Dalai Lama returned, "Being calm and being idle are too very different things. One can calmly put out a fire, or build a bridge."

"One can also enthusiastically do such things."

"Is that how you feel when you design holograms?"

Kenro looked longingly at an imaginary object. It was a holographic flower he had crafted for an important day. It wasn't any kind that had ever grown on Earth. It was his own creation. It had twenty-one petals, appearing in three layers: ten on the bottom, seven in the middle, four on the top. The stem and sepals were a deep purple, while the petals and stamen were bright pink, changing to aquamarine and scarlet red at timed intervals. It could be expanded in size so as to be used for a parade float. It was never used.

"Yes."

Elsewhere, Daniel Lockhart was walking down a hallway with Brian McDaniel and two armed bodyguards. They were in a hospital. Most of the electricity had gone out since the event—something to do with the tectonic shift. Brian noted the incessant flatline noises coming from many of the rooms.

"Can we bring any survivors?" Brian asked. Daniel looked back at the cytologist, saying, "Only a few, if any. We can't fit the whole world inside."

"I know. I don't like that."

"None of us do."

They turned past a corner and, upon doing so, spotted someone from afar. Daniel held a hand out, halting Brian. The bodyguards stopped as well. The stranger's arms hung, swinging like chains. His hands, however, were clenched fists. His eyes were covered by long hair, but their fury could be felt from a mile away.

"Sir?" Daniel called. The man lifted his head slightly. Brian trembled for a moment, then relaxed. If anything happened, *they* had the advantage.

"Sir?" he repeated. The man took a step in their direction. Daniel looked over at one of the bodyguards, who, in turn, looked at his partner and nodded. They both had their weapons at the ready. The man took another step their way, and another, and his appearance became more evident. He had been a patient there. His right ankle looked twisted, mangled. He nearly fell over several times. As he drew nearer, they could see his eyes and hear his low growling. Finally, he tried to lunge forth but his ankle stopped him. He yelped, spit dangling from his lips, hanging over the floor. His hands came up, clawing at the four like a—.

"Do it," Daniel ordered. The bullet soared down the hall. The first one didn't kill him. He fell over, beginning to beg for mercy, but not in any coherent language, only guttural snarls and howls. Daniel looked away. Brian did the same. He knew what had happened to this poor soul.

"Sir?" the shooter asked, not willing to fire again unless told to. Daniel couldn't watch as he quietly responded, "It's too late for him."

And the dog was put down.

"Why is calmness so important to you?"

The Dalai Lama smiled, replying, "It isn't."

"But you just defended it."

"Does that make it important?"

Kenro thought the matter over. It was clear to him the answer was "no," at least from his opponent's perspective.

"You don't want to be calm," began His Holiness, "because it feels unnatural at such a time to be calm. It has nothing to do with a want for enthusiasm. You look at the faces of the others in here and when you see their apprehension, you think that's the right thing to do."

Kenro rolled his eyes, "What, are you my therapist now?"

The Dalai Lama didn't look at him. His eyes were on another as he said, "It isn't wrong to feel angry, Mr. Chauren. At the least, it means you're still human."

"And what does that make you?"

The Dalai Lama didn't answer. His eyes remained on Klara Valentina, the Russian woman toward the front of the transport.

Daniel, Brian and the bodyguards passed two more turns. It was here they discovered a silent man clutching an infant in his hands, his face stained with tears. Brian went over to kneel beside him, placing a hand on his shoulder. Daniel was cautious in his approach, but he knew it was all right when the man didn't lash out.

"Are you all right?" the cytologist asked. The man didn't even look at him. He just kept staring at the baby. Brian looked at it. His heart sank. Daniel noticed it, too. That was why the man's eyes were drained.

"One of my men here can get you out safely," Lockhart stated. The man was still, petrified by his own child.

"He can have a proper burial later," Brian added, looking back to the father, who finally turned to the scientist. "Right now, you have to get out of here. Don't waste this chance."

The man looked over at one of the bodyguards. At first, uncertainty held him back. Then, after deciding there was no better alternative, he slowly stood up. Brian rose with him, moving the father beside his escort.

"This way," the bodyguard beckoned. They then departed to Daniel's transport outside.

When they were gone, Brian's guilt was revealed. He punched the nearest window of one of the patient rooms, cracking it. He then immediately vomited.

"Brian!" Daniel exclaimed, quickly grabbing the cytologist and supporting him. He coughed for a moment, then looked up at his friend.

"Daniel, I did that."

"Brian, stop."

"The interview, Daniel."

"The interview didn't kill anyone, got it? You didn't kill anyone."

"He looked newborn."

"Look at me, Brian."

He looked. Daniel kept holding on.

"You didn't kill *anyone*."

"But—."

"Brian."

He didn't say anything back. He wanted to agree with Daniel, but it was so difficult. Eventually he might get over it, but for now...

The Dalai Lama unbuckled his seat belt and stood up, moving around the seats to go speak with Klara. Kenro didn't pay him any mind. As the elder approached the politician, he smiled at her, nodding. She smiled back, or attempted to anyway.

"You're feeling well?" he asked, and with an air of humility, something she hadn't felt in some time, Klara answered, "Better. It still feels strange though, all of this."

"Good."

"Good?"

"It *should* feel strange."

Kenro had now turned to watch them from afar. After having synced the mouths of holographic humans to voice actors for so long, he could read lips, though only the Dalai Lama's face was visible to him.

"Why is that?" Klara said, looking at the faces of her fellow passengers. The Dalai Lama indicated the obvious, "It's strange."

Klara laughed a little at the simplicity of it, then agreed, "It *is*."

"I came here to ask something of you."

"Did you?"

"I did. My friend over there is being a bit pessimistic. I can hardly endure sitting beside him and I was just wondering if you wanted to trade seats with me."

"You want me to cheer him up?"

The Dalai Lama's eyes twinkled satisfactorily as he looked back at Kenro, answering, "I like that idea."

"Why not do it yourself?" Klara pointed out, and the Dalai Lama told her, "I need to take a nap."

The seat belt clicked and the ends slid apart.

"It's this one," Daniel said as the trio turned right. This was the hall. They stayed along the wall, looking out for any more threatening adversaries. When they reached the door, the bodyguard took point, aiming carefully as he swung it open. He surveyed the room before informing Daniel, "All clear."

Daniel immediately stepped inside. There, in bed, heart still beating, lungs still breathing, was Marcus Lockhart. The father's relieved sigh was very audible. He looked back at Brian, who was more than happy to see the child alive. If he'd somehow not survived...

But he *had* survived, and that was all that mattered. Daniel came beside him, looking to the cytologist and asking, "The patch..."

A neural patch rested on the boy's forehead. He was also hooked up to two drip feeds: one for food, one for water. Brian shook his head.

"Don't remove it yet," he said. "Wait until he wakes up. It'll be safer that way."

The other bodyguard was called via comlink. Once he was finished escorting the man with the baby, he would acquire the transport's emergency gurney and bring it to the waypoint sent to him—Marcus' room. As he waited, Daniel held his son's hand tenderly. They were almost out of this. Just a little longer and it'd be over.

"Brian."

"Yes?"

"We're going to make it."

"I know."

"I mean on Eden."

Brian still wasn't certain of it.

"We're going to make it," Daniel reiterated.

"We'll give it all we've got," said the cytologist.

Daniel gave a gentle squeeze to Marcus' hand and finished, "We'll have to give it more than what we've got."

Kenro was doing his best not to look at Klara when she spoke.

"He said you were," the Russian told him, again. Kenro retorted, "Well, he's wrong. I'm fine."

"I can usually tell when someone is wrong," she explained. The holographer replied, "Ah, yes, the quintessential trait of your kind: knowing when someone is wrong."

"Are we talking about Russians?"

"What do you think?"

"You think I did a bad job working with Mikhail?"

"I didn't pay much attention to the election."

"Enough apparently to compliment my talents. Daniel mentioned what you said to him when we met."

"It was the briefest of praises."

"But a praise nonetheless."

"I never said you were a bad politician," Kenro asserted, finally turning to her. "I just don't like that anyone who ever has the slightest disagreement with your stances on anything is immediately dubbed 'enemy' by you, thereafter bombarded with sound bites and propaganda and—."

"If I remember correctly," Klara cut him off, "the ratio of positive ads to negative ones used in our campaign was ten to three."

"And yet I remember the negative ones so well."

"Then they were effective," she told him. She paused before adding, "Sometimes you need to stick your hands in the mud before you can clean it up."

"And sometimes you can just clean it," Kenro riposted. Klara shook her head, sitting back, defeated.

"I'm not cheering you up, am I?" she asked, and the holographer's gaze fell elsewhere once again.

"I'm fine," he whispered.

Daniel was aboard the transport now, in the back with Marcus. The boy was lying in a small bed. His father's hand still grasped his. Brian was nearby, seated with the two bodyguards. He was quiet. They were all quiet.

There were a few survivors inside, those who had been discovered on the way out. Only seven, including the father they had found. He was still holding the tiny body, hoping it would raise its head and lift its eyelids. Nothing happened. The others were just ordinary people, some young, some old, all weary. They still couldn't believe what had taken place. One of them seemed more agitated than the rest. A watchful eye was kept on him.

Daniel looked over at the cytologist. None of it was his fault but, at the same time, if he hadn't gone on air, if he hadn't said what he said...

Brian only hoped it would all work out in the end. He hoped Eden would be a good home, a better home. Hope; it was as abundant as unscathed minds and untarnished souls, but it was all they had.

The hands stayed together. The points were clasped, sealed by paternal love. Amy was next to be picked up. He heard her voice over the comlink. He knew she was okay, but Marcus still hadn't...

"...awakened."

Kenro's interest had been redirected. The Russian held his attention now. She was talking about Man, about how, after such a catastrophic event, perhaps the curtain of unreason, insanity and violence had been lifted, about how Man might forget the old power struggles, wars and civil disputes, the uprisings and cultural differences, the politics, the greed. She spoke of how this sudden shift in what was important, though appalling   and dreadful in form, might have been just what Man needed to finally wake up. And Kenro, to a certain extent, agreed.

"Perhaps," he began to respond, "we will have stronger ties to one another thanks to all this, tighter bonds."

"At this point, anything is possible," said Klara, pleased with her progress. "Incidentally, do you happen to have any of your holograms on you?"

"Not here, I'm afraid. They're on archive loaders back home. They *can* be accessed wirelessly but not with a comlink. I talked with Leslie about it. She says they can be uploaded to the ship once we get there."

"At least they're safe."

Kenro seemed less overwhelmed by the situation regarding Earth. He nodded at Klara, telling her, "Right, I'm happy about that."

"Our new world will need a cultural foundation of some sort. Your art fits in with that perfectly."

The holographer smiled a little, replying, "Are you trying to get through to me?"

"I don't *try* to do anything, Mr. Chauren."

"Kenro."

"See?"

He chuckled at her. She chipped away at the geode. Tiny crystals were visible now, glowing vibrantly with color, truth and light. Collectively, they were a man, a creator, a thinker, an artist, a friend. *That* was Kenro, not some brooding, angry fellow who ignored the wise and denied amity from comrades.

"What brought you to America, Kenro?"

He didn't have to think twice. In a flash he remembered the poster and answered, "Freedom."

"A trite reason for journeying to the Land of the Free," Klara stated.

"Trite," the smiling holographer concurred, then adding, "but true."

"I suppose so."

They both spotted the Dalai Lama as he stood up, stretching his old bones. Kenro laughed a little, and Klara grinned.

"Well," she started, "I suppose that's my cue."

Kenro stuck his arm out, saying, "Wait until he gets over here."

"Oh? You'd rather I stayed?"

"I just wanted to ask what your contribution to our new world would be."

The Dalai Lama drew nearer as she thought it over. She smiled, responding, "Lingual diversity."

The two laughed, and the elder smiled. His little operative had done her job. *That* is when the child's eyes opened.

He blinked a few times, adjusting his vision to the dim interior. Only moments ago he had been walking with a stranger across snow-clad earth. Now the hum of an airborne transport en route somewhere filled his ears. He noticed drip feeds linked to him and wondered how he came to be in this condition. Memory gave him no guidance, so he was forced to investigate further. He put a small left hand to his head—right, he was a boy, a *young* boy—and felt for anything unusual. His fingers touched a patch of some kind. Bits and pieces of the past drifted back to him. There was a goldfish, and noise, and heat, and a knife, and a loving mother, and an honest father, and snow.

The boy looked around and saw a balding man seated far off. He was the type of fellow who would have appeared intelligent at first glance had he not been asleep and snoring vehemently. The youthful eyes might have scanned further on had the obvious not become apparent: something was holding his hand. It was a man, a familiar man. He looked an awful lot like the stranger the child was with before blacking out. He was sitting, napping, waiting for something. The boy shook the man's hand and, slowly, the lids came open.

22

At first it was shock that hit Daniel. His son didn't understand what the matter was. The man did not dare move, fearing that this was all simply a dream and that any sudden motions would wake him. But, after having pinched himself twice, it became clear that this wasn't just a dream. Dreams had never felt that real to Daniel, that good, that right. And Marcus couldn't help but remember...

"Daddy?"

That was all it took for the tears to flow like streams.

"So, Mr. Chauren," the Dalai Lama began, "is it too dark in here?"

Kenro smiled and answered, "I'd rather it were brighter."

PLAN

Home—home is a beautiful place. Home is where you know where everything is, where you know *what* everything is, *how* everything is. It's safe, warm, bright. It's stable, so you can return any time you like. It's personal, identifiable, honest. It reflects who you are and what you have the potential to become. It's yours. If an outsider attempts to take it from you, you make sure they don't, you hold your ground. That's how much you love it, how much you care. And now, just like that, it's gone. You stare at its smoking remains, miserable, not because it's been burned to the ground, but because as much as you'd like to think otherwise, you know who did it. You know who took away your home, and it wasn't an outsider.

Now, the six remained, directionless, stagnant.

Brian McDaniel, Leslie Thompson, Daniel Lockhart, Kenro Chauren, the Dalai Lama and Klara Valentina all sat in stunned, silent disbelief, having just finished viewing the news report from Multicast Worldwide over Daniel's comlink. It was worse than any of them could have imagined.

Apparently, the earthquake that had laid waste to the city they were standing within just moments ago, Los Angeles, was triggered by the eruption of the Yellowstone Caldera, a massive supervolcano that had lain dormant and looming as an ever present potential threat for many centuries.

The city was now nearly unrecognizable, mutilated, save a few street signs tumbling in the wind and the remnants of its many landmarks. The news stated that the force of the eruption was so strong that it caused a shift in Earth's tectonic plates. The Ring of Fire, as feared for so long, had been ignited, with most of the volcanoes along it now erupting, ejecting substantial amounts of ash into the air. The total amount of ash from all of the eruptions was predicted to block out the entire sky within the next few weeks and cause a long-term natural nuclear winter. The Armageddon that had been predicted for millennia had finally begun.

Five of the six sat in silence while the Dalai Lama stood, looking out at the destruction that had been brought to the city, to the world. He, too, remained silent for what seemed like eons. A single tear rested on the edge of his right eyelid, almost falling but still hanging on. He blinked, forcing it back in.

Grigory...

"How will we ever be able to recover from something like this?" Klara finally spoke up, attempting to shield the grief in her heart. "The odds seem completely out of our favor."

Recovery? The thought hadn't crossed any of the others' minds. It was impossible at this point, wasn't it? How could Earth be salvaged in such a state? How could the nations of the world be maintained, when the ground on which they stood would be little more than a memory soon enough?

"We won't," the Dalai Lama answered. The others looked at him, his back to them all.

"We," he began, "have been punished by a divine entity. The reason for this is simple: we allowed our world to become unbalanced. That is why a steel fist has slammed against us. This is our own doing. It could have been prevented. Our only chance now is to start anew. It will be a challenge without the appropriate resources, but we must try."

"How do we start anew on a dying planet?" Brian asked. All was quiet until Leslie broke the silence with, "We don't. We start on a new planet."

"And how exactly are we going to get to a planet that can support human life?" said Brian in disbelief, wondering how this notion of Leslie's had managed to come about. The planets nearby would've been suitable for enclosed colonies before but now, with Earth gone, the resources required to keep a colony perpetually stabilized were lost: oxygen, water, fertile soil, all soon gone within a matter of weeks.

"Project Eve," Leslie replied. "Normally I wouldn't be talking about this because it's highly classified, but, seeing as humanity is on the brink of extinction right now, I think it's only fair an exception be made."

All attention was directed at Leslie now. She continued.

"In 2040, back when the Federation was established, work began on this project. It involved finding a 'backup planet' in case this one was deep-sixed. It also involved building a ship to be used as a transport for up to fifteen hundred humans. This ship, the *Guardian*, was constructed in an underground silo. It's still down there being constantly maintained. We could use it to get to the backup planet they located in 2060, Eden."

Kenro wasn't satisfied, "How far off is Eden, exactly?"

"A little over two hundred and fifty light-years," the woman said. The holographer countered, "The kind of fuel it would take to—."

"It doesn't need much," Leslie interrupted. "It uses what's called a gravitational accelerator. Essentially, it has the ability to pull itself forward using the gravity of stellar bodies in front of it, while it repels itself from the gravity of those same sources as it passes them; it's a sort of slingshot effect. It does this extremely fast and could arrive at Eden in twenty to thirty years. All it takes is a bit of rocket fuel to start it up, and then off it goes."

Brian looked at Daniel uncertainly. Could they really pull this off?

"Though it sounds close to perfect," Klara began, rising to her feet, "I'm left wondering how one rebuilds humanity with just fifteen hundred people."

"Human embryos have been prepared and stored aboard the ship," said Leslie. "There are about nine thousand of them. They're meant to be raised on Eden. And that's not the end of it. There are embryos or the like for damn near every life form known to Man aboard the ship. They'll be used to create a balanced ecosystem for the newcomers."

She looked at Daniel, who gave her no returning gaze, and added, "You are aware of all this, aren't you?"

He was quiet for a moment. More of the dreaded noises of a city gone mad came about. Daniel could practically feel people digging their way out from underneath the rubble, if they could dig at all. Some had to be dragged out by friends, family, even strangers. Their shins might be splintered and protruding, their kneecaps crushed inward by debris. Would Hell be worse than this? Was there a Hell for those responsible to go to?

"I am," Daniel said, finally responding to her question. "That was back when my grandfather was in charge."

It was obvious, based on his tone of voice, that there were doubtful thoughts on his mind. Even so, Lockhart was slowly but surely being swayed into agreement.

With all this in mind, the Dalai Lama turned around and asked, "Are there *spirits* available to operate these bodies?"

Leslie grinned and answered, "Well, if spirits do exist, wouldn't you think they'd come aboard the ship with us knowing the world is coming to an end?"

The Dalai Lama smiled and nodded. An agreeable theory and to him, practical enough. For many hours the six talked, paced, sat, stood, shouted, paced more and sat again as they formulated an elaborate plan for the salvation of at least a portion of humanity. At last, it was set. Leslie would call upon a set of military transports to have them taken to the *Guardian*. The people who had followed the Dalai Lama throughout Los Angeles during his gathering would be brought to the ship as a large portion of those who would rebuild humanity. Though the original plan had selected specific individuals to do so, most (as confirmed by Multicast Worldwide) of these had been killed in the Yellowstone eruption, or in its aftermath. The crew of the *Guardian*, of course, would also be a part of the rebuilding group, as well as any living family members of the six present.

As all of this was being planned out, Daniel used his comlink to call and activate his private transport group. He had used it earlier to arrive with Brian and Kenro before meeting with Klara. He had to get Marcus and Amy and bring them to the *Guardian*, and quickly too. Though safety was within reach, danger was still afoot.

BURST

The caldera shook violently. Its engineered eruption would begin momentarily. Soon, a series of spectacularly horrifying events would be triggered by this devastating explosion. It was just a matter of time.

The faults in the land were rumbling. The electromagnetic energy firing upon it was *slowly* building a tremendous amount of volcanic pressure, ensuring the explosion would be as large as possible. The entire caldera was going to erupt, and it would be taking quite a few people with it to Kingdom Come.

The pressure was too great now. The nine hundred square mile mouth of the ancient supervolcano, just under the surface of Yellowstone National Park, would erupt right about—now.

Life for over a thousand miles was completely obliterated: plants, animals, humans, all extirpated during the event. The shock wave could be felt all across North America. People far out of range looked and saw the catastrophe occurring right before their eyes. A few of them thought it may have been an atomic explosion; they would soon be reeducated. The ash that would fall amounted to roughly nine feet in height. This ash would coat the entire continent.

The force of the explosion was so incredibly powerful, it caused a massive shift in the tectonic plates of the world. Though it would take a while for this shift to take full effect, it had already begun. There was no stopping it. This shift would set in motion something that had been feared for the longest time: the eruption of nearly every single volcano along the Ring of Fire. Mount Mayon, Mount Krakatau, you name it. They all went off, one by one, over the course of multiple weeks. The dust clouds that rose up from all of this volcanic activity would cover the entire sky, blocking out the sun. The stage was set and cataclysm struck. The Yellowstone Caldera's eruption would be forever remembered by any who survived it. The day it had been set off, February 7, 2121, would never be forgotten.

Armageddon had come.

FEAR

"Why aren't we firing?"

"We haven't received the code yet."

"Well, we'd better get it fast. The hyper-detector has picked up the energy signatures. The drones are headed our way."

Scalar: *having only magnitude, not direction.*

Weapon: *a thing designed or used for inflicting bodily harm or physical damage.*

Put the two terms together and you come up with a machine that uses electromagnetic energy to generate deadly results.

The team operating *Ivanovich*, the primary Russian scalar weapon, was very nervous as they sat in their control room. Dark Sword drones were soaring toward their position. Soon the enemy's railguns would tear their weapon apart.

"Where," the team chief, Viktor, began, "is that call? The President is supposed to contact us when he's ready."

Though English was the Federation's primary language, these men knew and spoke the old Russian tongue.

"He's probably speaking with his advisors about whether or not he should allow this," another, calmer team member,

Dominic, said. Viktor scoffed, "So he tells us to ready the weapon and *now* he's reconsidering it? Is he mad? The Greater Chinese satellites have obviously picked up the energy signature of *Ivanovich*. The goddamn drones are heading right for us!"

"Why don't we just fire it without his permission?" asked Leroy, a third member of the team. To this, Dominic replied, "We can't just use it. First of all, we'd be committing an act of treason and all be executed for it. Secondly, the President needs to send us the code to unlock the activation key receptacle. Then, we can use both keys at the activation center to fire the weapon. It needs to be actively firing for about sixty seconds to work."

Meanwhile, in the control room of the military command center operating the Dark Sword drones, the Chinese were defending an industrial facility that was producing key drone components. They had received information compiled nearly a decade ago from intelligence stating that if a scalar attack were to ever occur, this facility would be among the most likely targets. Command center personnel were shaking in their boots. Though their drones were drawing nearer and nearer to the scalar weapon, they were still in fear of the possibility of being too late.

Command center team leader Kun Lau sat intently, sweat pouring down the back of his neck, absolutely terrified of what was to come. He didn't even know if their contingency plan would work.

"Colonel Lau," a team worker called out, "our drones are exactly two hundred and eighty-five kilometers from their destination. They will begin firing at one hundred kilometers."

"Very good," Lau replied, just barely reassured by the man's words.

Near the industrial facility, another control room was being operated within by a powerful team. Their contingency plan was nearly ready. Just near the target of the scalar weapon was the electromagnetic tunneler, the redirection device that would send *Ivanovich's* attack directly to wherever they wanted it. Those operating in this room, though well prepared, were trembling, for they were not too sure if the tunneler's redirection efforts would be successful. The clock was ticking; time was running out.

"Dominic, how close are the drones?" Viktor asked back at *Ivanovich's* control room.

"Two hundred sixty kilometers out, sir," Dominic replied. They were really on edge now. They knew how close the enemies needed to be in order to fire their railguns. It was becoming far too dangerous.

"Where is our goddamn leader?!" Viktor cried, so stressed that his ears were beginning to ring.

In the drone control room, Colonel Lau was having mixed feelings of terror and high hopes. The drones were so close, and yet, *Ivanovich* was fully operational. What would happen? Who would win?

In the tunneler control room, redirection team leader Chen Gao sat with his eyes glued to the viewscreen before him. They had their own hyper-detector readied up. If the scalar weapon was fired on them, they'd be able to time their activation of the tunneler with the arrival of the energy wave. A nearly perfect plan was in place. But would it work? Would they be ready? Would they be quick enough to beat the Russians?

Viktor was seriously frantic now in the *Ivanovich* control center. It was only a matter of time before the drones arrived. They were just two hundred and five kilometers away from their destination, and one hundred and five kilometers from firing range. Suddenly, Viktor's comlink went off. He quickly checked the visual ID on it and in an instant he answered the call.

"Mr. President?" he said. "You have the code? Yes, I'll input it now. Thank you, Mr. President."

Viktor used the provided password to unlock the receptacle in which the keys were contained. With keys in hand, he called to Dominic and had him leave his station. With a trembling hand, Viktor threw one of the keys to him and they rushed to the activation center. When they arrived, the two locks were before them, spread apart just enough so one man could not simply use both keys himself.

"Ready?" Viktor asked. Dominic nodded, and then Viktor counted, "Three, two, one, NOW!"

They slid their keys into each one simultaneously, and turned them in the same fashion. At that moment, the weapon fired. The two stood shaking as the required time ticked away. It was the longest minute of their lives.

For a full sixty seconds the weapon fired without interruption.

The control room workers cheered wildly. They had done it! *Ivanovich* had been successfully fired. Their happiness was short lived, though. Soon after the weapon's firing, the control room rumbled violently. The railguns had begun their assault on the super weapon.

Meanwhile, the men working in the drone control room were aghast. Though they had destroyed *Ivanovich*, they had seen the energy wave it had fired off just beforehand. Colonel Lau was already on a secure comlink speaking with Chen Gao.

"Is the tunneler ready?" Lau asked, to which Chen replied, "We're timing it now. Don't worry."

On Chen's viewscreen he could see the energy wave coming closer and closer to them. He had his entire team ready for what was to come. He rubbed the sweat from his brow as he stared into the face of the enemy attack.

The closer it drew, the more their anxiety increased.

"Wait for it," Chen said, quivering. "Wait..."

Colonel Lau's fingers were crossed. He awaited his fate silently. The fear was overwhelming. It seemed so strange for silence to be this loud. Suddenly, his comlink went off. He answered it, and the words that came out of Chen Gao's mouth made him leap into the air and cheer:

"We did it."

The entire control room burst into a loud, happy uproar. It was incredible! *They* had won! Nothing else could take them by surprise at this point, for it had now been proven that the tunneler could and would be the bane of all scalar offenses! Lau had only one more question to ask Chen before he ended the call, "Mr. Gao, I must know one thing: where exactly was the blast redirected?"

Chen's reply was simply, "Are you familiar with the Yellowstone Caldera, sir?"

DIVISION

The mountainside rumbled as the doors to the hideaway slid open. The massive machine had a single orb on either side of it, with a huge connecting rod running between the two. This was the last act of war. This was *Ivanovich*.

In Los Angeles, at the historic Grauman's Chinese Theater, what had started as an impromptu media event had become an apparent vigil, with global media attention. Daniel Lockhart had just arrived alongside the relieved Klara Valentina. The proper arrangements had been made, and all was well concerning New Horizons. As he left their meeting, Daniel asked his friend if she would like to come with him to the theater. She accepted the offer out of sheer gratitude for his recent decision regarding the company.

In 2015, a stage had been implemented into the theater in order to hold concerts and play performances, rather than simply film premiers. Now, sitting upon this stage in a circular group, were Brian McDaniel, Kenro Chauren, and the Dalai Lama. The buzz of conversation going on throughout the building made it a bit difficult to hear what they were saying. The group the Dalai Lama had arrived with was growing. The people were laughing together, singing together, some even dancing together, giving each other comfort during these seemingly hopeless times. It's why he held this gathering. It's why he unified these people.

Daniel decided he'd go up on stage to meet with Brian, whom he was surprised to see speaking with His Holiness. Klara followed him. On Daniel's approach, the Dalai Lama said, "Hello, Mr. Lockhart. It is a pleasure to meet you. Brian tells me you're the reason he was able to do the interview on Fox Global."

Ivanovich's activation was beginning. Only a few more minutes and it would be ready to wreak havoc on the enemy. The electromagnetic energy flowed through it. The power that this machine held within was unrivaled.

"What is this event that is coming, Your Holiness?" Daniel asked the Dalai Lama. "What do you see?"

He and Klara were now seated with the others.

"I am no prophet, Mr. Lockhart," the elder began. "I am simply another ordinary man, like you. The only difference between you and I—and it is minute—is my willingness to allow balance to exist. It is a trait most people lose as their bodies age, but still remains within us all, if only faintly. There are those who would see our 'enemies' destroyed. But there are no enemies, only those who have lost their way, the ones who have tipped the scales. We must realign them."

The target was locked. The weapon was nearly ready. *Ivanovich* was about to help Tangshan re-experience an event from its past. The quake was coming.

"All I can say," the Dalai Lama went on, "is that there is a catalyst here, on this planet. It will trigger the event I have spoken of. As I said before, I do not know whether it is in our favor or not..."

The energy wave would have to travel through hundreds of trillions of *infinitesimal* gaps between the nucleus and orbiting electrons of countless atoms along the way, but it would reach its target. This wave could literally move through *any substance known to Man. Ivanovich* would be fully operational in ten, nine, eight...

"...but what I do know is this..."

...seven, six, five...

"...no matter what happens..."

...four, three...

"...so long as we remain united..."

...two...

"...we will survive."

...one.

After the Dalai Lama had spoken, Daniel began looking out into the crowd. He spotted Leslie Thompson, the woman who had helped him confess about his son. Why she was at the theater?

"Leslie!" he called. She heard him and turned to the stage. He waved a hand, beckoning her. A small smile grew on her mouth. This wasn't a fruitless undertaking after all.

"Why aren't we firing?" said a man, somewhere.

"We haven't received the code yet," said a man, someplace.

PINPOINT

The President of the Russian half of the United Federation, Nikolai, was very concerned. As he sat within his office in the Kremlin, he could not stop thinking about how close Greater China was to cutting off the entire eastern half of his country. Their Dark Sword drones were the real threat. They flew too fast, too high, and were extremely maneuverable. Their railguns, however, made the *biggest* difference.

A crack sounded. Nikolai jerked his head about, seeking the noise's source. Could he see it? Nothing was there, not a mouse, not a roach—nothing. He slowly relaxed again, but only just. He wasn't anxious about tiny sounds because of drones and Greater China; the *internal* conflict had brought that. Lately, even his highest ranking military officers had been at odds, and not just verbally. Only two days before he had passed by a colonel with a black eye and swollen lips. He had attempted to handle these brawls diplomatically, but they persisted regardless.

It would be over soon, the fighting.

Finally, the leader's wait ended as a courier entered the room. The man was grinning as he stepped before Nikolai and stated, in English, "Mr. President, we've found it."

"What?" Nikolai asked in the same language, seeming brighter already.

"Sir," the courier began, "we've discovered that the heart of the military complex producing key components for the Dark Sword drones is in Tangshan, in Hebei Province."

Relief made the President's eyes glow. He now relaxed entirely, a smile dawning on him. How those words soothed him.

"I have also," the courier continued, "been ordered to mention that this is the same location of the second most deadly earthquake in world history."

"Yes, yes!" the President cried, looking at the ceiling from his seat. "A weakness! We've finally found one! This will turn the tide, I'm sure of it."

"As am I, sir."

A fact had gone unaddressed. Nikolai noticed.

"Wait..."

"Yes, sir?"

"Why were you ordered to tell me about the earthquake?"

The courier grinned as he said, "You tell me, Mr. President."

Nikolai had his realization and chuckled, then telling the courier, "Ripe for seismic activity, eh? I'll speak with the engineers in Facility 26 soon. I'll have them ready Big Ivan."

"Very good, sir," the messenger said. After that, he departed. This was the beginning of the event the Dalai Lama had spoken of, the event that would change everything.

TOUCH

The Dalai Lama was walking through the streets of Los Angeles, his security team close behind him as his robe billowed in the wind. He looked about at the frightened people passing by him. He knew what was on their minds. The thought of these two superpowers eradicating one another wasn't an easy one to stomach. Help was what they needed right now, a hand through the dark, a gentle one, a wise one.

The press had been following him for hours. They had waited outside the hotel room he'd checked into that morning. He wanted to take his daily walk, whether the press followed him or not. He made a promise to all of the reporters that once he finished his walk he'd answer all of their questions.

After some time moving about, the elder had gathered quite a few followers. He did not ask them to follow him, it was their own choice. Perhaps they wanted to know where he was off to, or maybe being in his presence just seemed comforting. He was now moving along Hollywood Boulevard, within the renovated area of Old Hollywood, when his eyes fell upon the historic Grauman's Chinese Theater. His group of followers was growing large at that point, so he decided to enter the building. It was easy to deal with the theater attendants. When he asked if he could hold a gathering there, the awed employees told him they'd make reasonable arrangements.

Soon enough everyone who had followed the Dalai Lama was seated in the theater (most of whom had purchased bags of popcorn and other forms of classic theater food). The elder was standing on stage, and the reporters, along with his astonished security team, were gathered in the front rows of the audience. This was quite the impromptu press conference His Holiness was holding. That was all right though. Their live streaming cameras were already transferring the footage to their respective multicasts. It was at this point that the Dalai Lama raised his hand. In an instant the crowd was hushed.

"I shall now take your questions," the elder said, loudly, as he waved a hand across the reporter filled rows. Many hands rose into the air, and the Dalai Lama pointed at one.

"Your Holiness," the selected reporter began, "what are your thoughts on the conflict between Greater China and the United Federation? Are you favoring either side?"

"I favor no sides," the Dalai Lama replied, "in any conflict. As far as I am concerned, *balance* is what needs to be maintained. And regarding the conflict itself, I don't believe much needs to be said of it. Look at the people in this room. Look at their faces and tell me what you believe *they* think of this fighting. Good people, the innocent, do not wish for war to be a part of their lives. I believe that I am a good person. Therefore, it is easy to tell what I think of it."

More hands were raised and he pointed to another, a woman this time. She asked him, "What do you think of the recent Fox Global interview with Brian McDaniel, the cytologist? Do you have any disagreements with it?"

"What is it that I've been fighting for?" the Dalai Lama said. "Spirituality is a thing the entire world should know to be true. Anything in support of that I myself am supportive of. If a dispassionate scientist can find signs that there is a soul, that Man is not just meat and bones, then we are on the right track."

Another reporter was selected, who asked, "Do you feel this conflict is the result of the worldwide aggression, or is that an unrelated issue?"

"There are no accidents," the elder said. "Everything is tied together in some way."

Finally, the question he had been waiting for was asked by the next selected reporter, who said, "Why have you brought us here?"

The Dalai Lama had only just caught that, for his ears were still adjusting to the surgery. He smiled softly, his eyes twinkling, and said, "At first, I believed I had come to this place, America, to find someone. However, I know now why I have truly come here. I am here to unite the people of this nation, and of all nations. One might be wondering if this is the end for us. Is it? I do not know. But I do know this: the time for us to come together, in peaceful unity, is now.

"I feel in my heart that an event that will change us all is coming," he went on. "It may be in our favor. It may not. In either case, I have a single request: do not let this madness that has come about take you, for it will only make any possible downfall more likely. Be strong, be firm, and together we will make it through these dark days."

The beauty of multicast reporting was how easy it was to witness events like this one. Leslie witnessed it. Daniel, Brian and Kenro witnessed it. Even Klara saw the entire thing. And they all agreed with it. Not only that, but they all wanted to go to this gathering and be beside the Dalai Lama when whatever this event was came to pass. Daniel called up Klara, telling her they had to change the location of their meeting to Los Angeles. He would be bringing Brian and Kenro with him.

Leslie was sitting alone in her new office at Edwards Air Force Base, watching the above events unfold on her comlink, when her stream was interrupted. She looked quizzically at it. She hadn't expected a call. She checked the ID: Pearl Harbor.

The colonel tensed up. The news was out about that already: history repeating itself in a new manner. Descending through water, the images on screens—she remembered them. He wasn't in any of the footage though, and when she'd called before, when she'd asked...

They wouldn't tell her anything last time, just that he was okay. It was still ringing, awaiting her touch. She took a deep breath, accepted the call, and held the device to her ear.

"Hello?"

"Colonel Thompson?"

"Yes?"

She just listened. No talking, no interruptions, just listening. She answered where needed with only a word or two, and then finally, when it was done, she told the man on the other end, "Thank you."

It was the weakest thanks she'd ever given. She let the comlink rest on her desk and just sat there, staring at it. Steps passed by her door, men in boots, off to follow orders. She wanted to cry, but she hadn't cried since she was a little girl. Crying wasn't even a thing to her anymore. At most it was a memory, like Chet.

It felt like the phone was still ringing, like she was stuck in that stupid memory. The boots trailed off. Angry memories came now, memories of her being forced to do things she hated, betraying herself, memories of being dragged away from loved ones by duty, by war, memories that made her want them dead, all of them, not just the Greater Chinese, General Cameron, too, and the Presidents, and Klara Valentina, and the *whole damned planet*, until EVERY ONE OF THEM WAS—!

And then, she felt a warmth upon her shoulder. She realized then that her right hand had been clenched into a fist. It slowly unfurled as her anger died. She put her other hand to the warm shoulder, and a feeling of certainty touched her mind, like words without a voice reaching her ears.

"I know," she whispered, and then, and as the drips landed on her lap, she decided it was time she joined the others in Los Angeles, regardless of whatever punishment she might incur.

The six would be together.

DESPERATION

The Presidents of both the Russian and American halves of the United Federation were sitting in their respective countries, talking over a secure comlink. The American President, Malcolm Jennings, was just about to take a much needed vacation to Jackson Hole, in Wyoming, when he received a call from his Russian counterpart. They were now having a most delicate discussion.

"Drastic action must be taken, Malcolm. We are a in a perilous situation. After the decimation of Vladivostok, the Chinese have moved further north. They've taken Khabarovsk, Malcolm. They're too powerful. Legions of troops are marching through Russian cities every day. Something must be done."

"Look, Nikolai," Malcolm began, "you aren't the only one having problems. We *both* received reports that the naval base at Pearl Harbor was attacked and *destroyed* by Dark Sword drones. They used goddamn railguns against us! Nearly everyone there was killed! How the hell do you think the American people are feeling about this? The heart of liberty was practically torn out!"

"All the more reason to use the scalar weapons *now*, while we have a chance."

The American President sighed and told his partner, "We could risk causing a national uproar."

"It can't be as bad as what happened after your little space assault," Nikolai told him. Malcolm then continued, "We can't do this. It's too dangerous. A scalar war could erupt from it.

What if those rumors we heard about the redirection devices years back were true?"

"There is no hard evidence that those devices ever existed. If they had been built, we would have found out by now."

Silence ensued for a few moments, broken by Nikolai with, "There's always the *Guardian*, Malcolm."

"I won't accept something like that happening," Malcolm snapped.

"I only mentioned it because you're afraid. You don't honestly think an apocalypse will spawn from a scalar war, do you?"

Malcolm was shaking his head as he responded, "I don't know. I'm just worried, that's all."

"Listen," Nikolai began, "I'll do what I have to. I need to defend my country. So do you. Do what you wish, but once I have a target, I'm using the weapon."

Malcolm did not argue with the Russian President, he merely said to him, "If I have to, I may do the same. But I'm not risking it right now. You do what you want, but don't use it a second time unless they continue marching through after the first strike."

"We'll see what happens," was Nikolai's reply. That was all that was said. Malcolm was then on his way to Jackson Hole, just eighty-two miles from...

CRACKING

Klara was in awe at the sight before her. Watching her candidate, Mikhail, pack his things in his hotel room was much like watching a superhero give in just as he's about to defeat the villain and get the damsel. What the hell was he thinking?

"Mikhail," she began, her mouth agape, even between phrases, "I don't understand. You have this race in the bag. What's wrong? Why are you quitting?"

The candidate just kept packing his bags, seeming completely oblivious to her being there.

"Look at the polls," she went on. "You're beating out Nikolai! We've nearly got a landslide going at this point. We don't have much further to go, so if you'd please just..."

No results came. He was like a machine, completely ignoring her, just going through the motions. Klara finally shook her head and decided she wasn't going to let this continue. She stomped over to Mikhail and spoke loudly and firmly in his ear—in the old language, no less.

"You are going to explain yourself, right now! If you don't, I'll—!"

"I am going to Jackson Hole," he retorted just as firmly. "I have friends waiting there for me. I am done with this race. It is not worth it. I can't go on like this and I need a break. We're done."

"You aren't even sorry you're leaving? You're just going to walk off? This affects me, too, Mikhail. If you would just reconsider..."

He had finished packing and was already headed for the door. Klara got between him and his objective. She then saw a fire that she hadn't seen before burning in Mikhail's eyes. He gripped her shoulder and shoved the woman aside. She gasped, but it left no impression on the man. He just went on his way out of the room, off to Jackson Hole.

Klara fell to her knees. It was quiet now. There were still footsteps coming from the hall outside, but they faded. There was nothing now, no one, just her. The tips of her fingers quivered. She couldn't think of anything to do, anything to say to the empty air. She just breathed. Though her mind darted about like a fly on fruit, her eyes remained fixed on the floor. She had reached the bottom. So, this was what it was like to lose? And all this time she had thought failure was impossible, an unreachable condition for someone such as her.

Oh, but she could run a company while campaigning, couldn't she? New Horizons was a piece of cake, wasn't it? In the beginning it was fine, sure. But something happened along the way. Perhaps it had something to do with what Brian talked about in that interview. Had it gotten that bad? Had the aggression gotten to her? Oh, God. If it had...

It was in these hopeless thoughts that the call from Daniel Lockhart came.

ESCALATION

Daniel was once again sitting beside his son in the hospital. His eyes rested on the vitality monitor just beside the bed. The boy hadn't awoken in so long. Just watching him lie there made his father's stomach turn. Yes, there was war, there was fire, there was impending doom, but none of it meant anything anymore. Guilt kept him *here* of all places, guilt and love. His eyes stayed on the monitor.

The door of the room opened and a nurse stood within the threshold. He had asked her to let him know when his guest arrived. She spoke, "The cytologist is here, Mr. Lockhart. He's brought someone with him."

"Who?" he asked, to which she replied, "Kenro Chauren, sir."

"The holographer?"

"Yes, sir."

"Really? Well, send them in."

The Oscar winning holographer? What was *he* doing there, with Brian no less? The nurse left, and only a few minutes passed before both men arrived. Brian introduced Daniel to Kenro and explained how they'd come to know each other as friends. There were three other chairs in the room up against a wall. They pulled two of them to the bed and sat down.

"So, this is your son?" Brian asked.

"Yes," Daniel answered. "He's one of the reasons I called you here. I need to know something, Brian."

"Go right ahead."

"I need to know..."

Brian listened.

"I just..."

Brian still listened.

"I'm sorry, this is a bit—."

"It's fine. Take your time, Daniel."

Kenro watched to two interact. The frankness of their words was unexpected.

"Thanks, sorry. Brian, the interview made it pretty obvious that you've done quite a bit of work in neuroscience alongside cytology."

"This is about the boy's thoughts?"

"I need to know if the aggression will remain with Marcus after he wakes."

Brian sighed and told him, "It's impossible to say. The chances of it leaving him aren't significantly high. However, there is a slight possibility that the concussion has damaged his cellular brain pattern in such a way that it would end the effect."

"How did you know it was a concussion that put him here?" said Daniel. Brian's eyes remained on the boy as he replied,

"Well, the giant neural massage patch on his head may have assisted me in forming my conclusion."

Kenro chuckled, Daniel smiling slightly. Then the holographer asked, "Forgive me for asking, Mr. Lockhart, but isn't this a conversation you could've had over the comlink?"

"If Marcus wakes up, and he's okay mentally, Brian needs to be here. I want him running checks on my son's patterns, like he did with the Caretaker subjects. I need to *know* this won't happen again."

Brian nodded. After all this man had done for him, he was willing to give forth this small payment.

"Also," Lockhart said solemnly. He looked to the viewscreen on the wall of the room and called out, "Record 551."

As the screen began scrolling through its recorded shows, Daniel told his guests, "I decided to have this afternoon's BBC News multicast recorded. Have either of you seen or heard of it? It ended just recently."

Both of them shook their heads, and Daniel said, "Good, then this won't be a waste of your time."

They all watched as the recorded program played.

"Good afternoon, everyone," the anchorperson began. "I'm Todd Benson, and today we have very alarming news to deliver. To begin, this morning a press conference was held in Beijing by the Supreme Chairman of Greater China. It entails a declaration we here at the BBC thought would never come about: war between the Federation and Greater China. We have our senior correspondent, Susan Linn, with more about this stunning development."

The screen cut to Susan Linn, who briefly described what had happened at the press conference. Then she introduced an excerpt from the event.

Around a hundred reporters sat before the podium at the conference. Behind the podium was the Supreme Chairman himself. He had begun his speech some time ago, and was now delivering an important point.

"I am absolutely appalled," he began, "by the naked assault that has just been perpetrated on our proud nation. Exactly seven hours ago, I received reports that *dozens* of Greater Chinese commercial satellites were disrupted by a particle beam fired from a United Federation ship. This is an outrage, and must be *severely* punished!"

The screen cut back to the anchorman, who told his viewers, "That was just the beginning of events involving this new conflict. We have received reports of gunfire and explosions being heard just outside the Russian port city of Vladivostok. We will now go live to our Russian correspondent, Zhev Pavok, to learn more."

Kenro shifted uncomfortably in his seat.

The multicast had now cut to a snow covered area. Zhev Pavok was crouched low, as was his cameraman. They watched from afar as waves of Chinese soldiers attacked a smaller number of Russian infantry.

"Thank you, Todd," the correspondent whispered. "I'm here just outside Vladivostok. Right now, as I'm speaking, the fighting between the United Federation and Greater China has begun. This could be the first of many battles fought between the two sides of this conflict."

"Stop," Daniel called out. The screen went blank. Both Brian and Kenro turned to the man, who told them, "The rest is a bit too—it isn't necessary, just more..."

"I understand," Brian said. Daniel sighed and told him, "That ship that attacked those satellites was the *Vanguard*. It's owned by Starbound Enterprises, which is under New Horizons."

"Klara allowed this to happen?" Brian asked, to which Daniel replied, "She's having trouble juggling her political career and her job as chairwoman. The Russian military's been taking advantage of her confusion and, in doing so, adding to it. They're crawling all over the company. She just flew over to see Mikhail about his decision to drop out of the election. I don't know what to do about it."

Kenro finally spoke up, "Mr. Lockhart, I understand that you wish to look after your son. He is a beautiful boy, and I can see how much you care. However, I must state how much I believe that you should return to New Horizons. I don't think you need me to explain to you why you're needed there now more than ever. This world is becoming more and more chaotic by the second, and, whether you like it or not, your absence is contributing to it by allowing Klara to go on there. She may be a good politician, but she can't replace you. You need to step in and retake what is rightfully yours."

Daniel disagreed, "I'm not fit to do that right now, Mr. Chauren."

"And she is, Mr. Lockhart?"

"It's better than what I'd be doing."

"She can't focus at all."

54

"Neither can I."

"Why?"

Nothing was said, and then, "Shut up."

"Mr. Lock—?"

"Shut up!"

His voice: Daniel hadn't even noticed its sudden rise in volume. The other two stared with wide eyes. Daniel realized what was going on and relaxed. He thought he heard something, but it wasn't there anymore.

"I..." he tried to begin, but nothing else came. Brian looked over at Kenro. The holographer's gaze was fixed on the father before him.

"Mr. Lockhart, I—."

"You're right."

Brian and Kenro exchanged glances, then looked back at the man. What had he said?

"You're right," he repeated in a whisper. "I can't let it win. I can't let it beat me."

Daniel looked at his son and continued, "I have to do it, for him. I have to call Klara. I have to return to the Board."

Kenro leaned back in the chair, while Brian leaned forward.

"I have to get things back on track," were Daniel's last words before making the call.

BETRAYAL

The Dalai Lama was once again in the office of his old friend, Grigory Yaroslav, head of Russian Internal Security. Only a few hours ago, the Dalai Lama had received eardrum surgery. He was now adjusting to it, listening as intently as he could to what was being said.

"I'm sorry, Jianyu," Grigory began, "but I cannot offer the RIS's services any longer. Our losses have been growing since the attack. Though the entire country is a target, we have been specified as the ones assisting you."

"Grigory," the Dalai Lama said nervously, "you are the only one who can help me. Without you, I cannot regain my influence within Greater China. The people will lose faith in me. They will believe I have given up."

Grigory instantly became agitated, "I have told you already, I cannot have the RIS focused on such an insignificant campaign."

The Dalai Lama's countenance went from anxious to bewildered. The change in his friend was...

"Insignificant? Is there something wrong, Grigory? Please, tell me."

"Get out."

"What?"

"Get out of my office," Grigory growled. "I don't want to see you here again."

"Grigory, I'm your friend. Please, just—."

"Leave, Jianyu!"

The Dalai Lama recalled the Fox Global interview. The cytologist was right. Perhaps what he'd spoken of *was* causing the worldwide aggression. Grigory would never act like this toward the Dalai Lama under any other circumstances. He was being altered.

Upon leaving the Prime Compound, the Dalai Lama realized what he had to do. He needed to find Brian McDaniel. He needed to talk to him about what was going on, and ask if there was some way of reversing this mass effect other than that which was previously stated.

ADDRESS

The crowd was on Klara's side. It was a massive congregation, probably about thirty thousand people. They cheered as she raved on and on about the commitments Mikhail would be making toward both halves of the Federation, and how he would be not just a great leader, but one of the best the Federation would ever know.

"And, of course, I must address one final issue," she began as the crowd grew quiet. "I have heard, as I've gone about speaking to constituents across both continents, that there is worry of secrecy. This worry has obviously been caused by the wrongdoings of the recently passed Markev Gaofenburg. I am here to tell you today that *no* action will be taken by Mikhail Gavrikov, or the Russian House, without the *entire* Federation being fully aware of it. All meetings between the House and Gavrikov will be viewable via a new multicast designed specifically for the purpose of transparency."

The crowd was once again going wild. Klara Valentina had won them over, every last one of them. As the sound died down, which took some time, she continued.

"The reason for this is not just because of the mistakes of a former leader, however. In my heart I feel that it is for the sake of becoming more unified. I have seen tension throughout the Federation since Gaofenburg left office. Even our current Nikolai seems to have skeletons hidden somewhere. This new multicast, I feel, will alleviate that tension. If we are to coexist peacefully, we must become more open to each other. As I leave here, I offer that very thing. Good night, good luck, and God bless the United Federation."

She smiled and waved as she went backstage to be taken to her transport by security. The crowd was going nuts. It was incredible. She had done it! She felt so triumphant, so powerful. There wasn't anything that could possibly stop her and Mikhail from winning the election now.

"Miss Valentina?"

Klara turned around. A security guard was holding a comlink in his hand.

"It's for you," he told her as he handed it over. She held it to her ear.

"Yes?" she said. "Who is this?"

"Klara," a voice uttered, slowly. "He's done."

"Joseph? Is that you? Who's done? What's wrong?"

"It's Mikhail, Klara," he told her.

"Yes, what about him?"

More silence, then: "He's pulled out. He's finished."

Klara stopped dead in her tracks. The comlink fell from her fingers and hit the ground with a thud.

"Miss Valentina?"

Her face grew pale.

"Miss?"

The guard picked up the fallen comlink and spoke into it, "Sir? No, she's all right."

She wasn't.

"I'll ask. Miss Valentina, Mr. Danshov wishes to know what your next course of action will be."

Victory was so close.

"Miss Valentina?"

Why did he just...?

"Klara?"

"The pilot..." she whispered.

"I'm sorry?"

"Contact the pilot," she ordered. "Let him know we are not going back to Washington."

"Yes, Miss Valentina," the guard responded. He left. Klara didn't *try* to do anything. She'd get through to Mikhail. It might take some doing, but she would.

She always did.

WARBOUND

"A particle beam?"

Leslie watched as the weapon was installed into the belly of the *Vanguard* by tech specialists. The ship had what looked like old fashion bomb bay doors hanging open for the beam to be loaded in. Leslie was still astonished by the idea of a ship designed for exploration being used for combat. This wasn't right.

"And you want me to lead the crew?" she asked General Isaac Cameron. "I don't even know how this thing works."

"It's an ultra-high energy weapon," Isaac began. "It fires electrons at any selected target and disrupts the molecular structure of said target. Simple enough, Colonel Thompson?"

"What are we shooting at?"

"What you're ordered to."

"General, I'll need more than that."

Cameron was reluctant to reveal the details, but he knew now was as good a time as any.

"You'll be provided with a list of Greater Chinese satellites," he replied. "You'll find them, take them out, then return and be debriefed."

The colonel thinned her eyes, "We're going to war?"

"We are."

"General, we couldn't possibly have any good reason to attack the—."

"We have two."

"What are they?"

"That's for me to know."

Leslie glared at him, "And me? Can you at least tell me where the intel came from?"

The man was frustrated, "Thompson, don't question the situation at hand. You're needed. You've been helpful in wartime before."

To this came the response, "I knew what we were fighting for before. I'm not going to allow my ship to be turned into a weapon, especially under these conditions. With all due respect, sir, this is unacceptable."

"I wouldn't worry about pulling the trigger," General Cameron told her. "That's his job."

He pointed to a man in a black uniform with red stars on either shoulder. Leslie frowned and said, "I don't care who's 'pulling the trigger,' General. I won't be a part of this."

"Unless you'd like to be brought in front of a court-martial, you will do as you're told, *Colonel*. Do you understand?"

A thousand curses were stayed at Leslie's lips. If she were not so circumspect, she might have torn him a new one. Instead, there came an averse, "Yes, sir."

After that, she left him and began walking toward the boarding walkway of the *Vanguard*. She could've declined. She could've chosen a military court over what she'd be doing now. Why pick the latter? Did she not have the fortitude to do what she felt was right, to stand her ground in the face of adversity? Of course she did. She knew the weight her rank carried, and she knew it wasn't worth wasting in order to prolong the inevitable. Someone else would lead the crew in her absence, *if* she were absent. Better to sacrifice her morals now so that her title might be put to good use later.

Her comlink went off. She stopped and took a look. After accepting the call, she raised it to her ear.

"Chet," she said.

"Hey," he responded. The voice of a friend is really something once the face leaves you. Since before enlisting, she'd known that face: the chestnut brown, messy hair, the freckles that lived on throughout his aging, if but faintly, and the kindness of his eyes. He wasn't just her best friend; he was the brother she never had. And now they were separated by unkind circumstances.

"What is it?" she inquired. "Can it wait? I'm about to get aboard."

"Uh," Chet started, deciding. "I guess it can. I was really just calling to check in, see how it's going."

"Terribly."

"I had a feeling."

"You?"

"It can wait, if you have to—."

"Just talk to me."

"I'm fine. We're working on getting these ships tested for underwater exploration."

"On other planets?"

"Yeah, it's actually pretty neat."

"Neat?"

"Shut up, Leslie."

"I didn't know people still used it that way."

"You don't know a lot of things."

"When do you get back to Starbound?" she asked, moving further into the ship. Chet answered, "I don't know. They haven't told me everything yet."

"Well, once you know, tell me, okay?"

"I will."

"I'll find a way back."

"I know you will."

"Okay, we'll talk again later."

"Right," he replied, then adding, "Wait, when?"

"Later," she told him, and Chet said, "Okay. Later."

That was it. That was when she hung up. From that point forth, Leslie had lost her brother's voice.

FRIEND

Brian's head was in his hands. He was sitting in his now empty archive room at the lab. How could he have let this happen? Everything was crashing down and he feared it was entirely his fault. He should never have stepped in front of that camera. He should never have spoken with Valentina. He should never have begun his side project. It was all one big mistake. Then, a knock came at the door. He opened it. An assistant of his was standing there.

"Someone is here to see you, Mr. McDaniel," she told him. "He's come here all the way from Greater China."

Brian was highly surprised. Someone fled the country during a time like this just to see him? Who could this man possibly be?

"Send him in," Brian said. He closed the door and sat back down. He wanted to do something, but what was there to do? Nothing was fixable at this point. It had all come apart since the interview, since the breach. Wait, could this visitor be a— ah, no, couldn't be. They wouldn't have gotten through the security checks downstairs if they had anything to do with the military on the other end of the world. They would have been arrested immediately for war crimes, whether they had committed any or not.

Only moments later, another knock came and the cytologist opened the door. The visitor bowed low and smiled at him.

"Kenro Chauren?" Brian cried. "What in God's name are you doing visiting me?"

"Just looking for guidance," Kenro replied, smiling sadly. Much pain rested behind those eyes. The cytologist gestured for Kenro to enter the archive room and sit in the chair opposite his. Then, their conversation began.

"So," the holographer began, "this is where you keep all your records?"

"*Kept*," Brian corrected. "My archive loader was raided along with my hard copy documents. I'm not at liberty to say too much, but I don't think it matters who stole it or why. The fact is the data's gone."

Kenro frowned as he said, "Is there any way I can help?"

Brian chuckled a bit and said, "Let bygones be bygones."

Kenro didn't know exactly where he was going with this. He was trying to find something proper to say. That's when Brian asked him, "So how did you get here? It couldn't have been easy getting out of Greater China during these stressful times."

"It's not as hard as it seems," the holographer said. "I have a few friends left back there who were able to get me out."

"I see."

Kenro was surprised. He expected a much livelier man. He had just made history with his interview. Why was he so depressed? His lab had been raided, but this seemed deeper than that. Something else was wrong.

"Mr. McDaniel," Kenro said, "forgive me for asking, but is there something else troubling you?"

Brian let a doleful sigh exit. He would be blunt.

"Well," Brian began, "to put it simply, it may be possible that I've started a war between Greater China and the United Federation."

Kenro's eyes widened as he said, "That's rather alarming, Mr. McDaniel."

"I know, and it's all because of that damn interview. I'm sorry it ever happened."

"With all due respect, Mr. McDaniel, I thought your interview was sensational."

Brian tried to smile about it. He failed miserably.

"I'm glad you feel that way," he said. "It's not the interview in and of itself that was destructive, just the things it led to. In all honesty, Mr. Chauren, I think I need guidance more than you do right now."

"Please, call me Kenro, Mr. McDaniel," the holographer told him. The cytologist, with tired eyes, replied, "Brian's fine."

Kenro nodded in agreement. He had come for help, and he had received it in the form of a new goal: aiding this man. It was true that Brian needed guidance, maybe more than Kenro did.

"What will you do now?" Kenro asked willfully. Brian shrugged.

"Wait?" he said inquisitively. "I don't really know what for though."

"Maybe you should apply that law you spoke of," the holographer told Brian. "It seems to have proven itself true."

"What, about the agreement?" Brian chuckled. "I'm afraid it'll probably take more than prayers to fix this mess."

"Not prayers, Brian," said Chauren, waving his hand, "just simple agreement. Simple, certain agreement might bring it about. No doubts, no reservations. It's worth a shot."

Such a simple idea, Brian thought. Foolish, childish, and simple, that's what that was. Things like that don't just work. There's more to it than that. And yet, the more he thought about it, the less absurd the idea became, and then more absurd, then less, more, less, more, until he finally smiled, raised both eyebrows and said, "You know, it may be worth a try. I haven't got much to lose, anyhow. It probably won't work, but..."

He stopped himself. *Just do it*, he thought. *Just go all in.* Then his eyes closed, and he imagined some catalyst coming to assist him in this time. Of course, nothing happened. He went on like that for a few minutes, snorting with laughter. When he opened his eyes, there was still nothing. He closed them again and kept repeating the action over and over. Kenro looked around hopefully after the third repetition: nothing. There was no laughter now, only a bitter scientist and an artist whose optimism was dying fast.

Just go all in.

The cytologist gritted his teeth. He was so infuriated with the nothingness that he stood up. And then, without a doubt, without a reservation, without a stutter, he spoke in a crescendo:

"Damn it, universe, *you're* going to listen to *me* for once. I'm tired of you treating me like dry dirt. I'm tired of you taking without giving. I'm tired of you being cold and cruel to us just because we're smaller than you! It's time you helped us out a little bit! It's time you stopped being such an asshole! Now, make something happen, or, I swear to whatever made you, I'll split every single one of your *goddamn atoms* until there's nothing left of you, not a dust particle, not an electron, *nothing*! *You hear me*?!"

The cytologist's comlink sang a tune, a tune of change. The men looked at each other, somewhat shocked. Kenro was beaming, seeing Brian's newly injected passion as the cause of the call. The scientist answered, and a smile broke out on his face when he heard the familiar voice.

It was Daniel Lockhart.

FAREWELL

"Do you really have to leave?" Chet asked. Leslie smiled at her friend weakly, the future uncertain. She continued packing.

"I've been away from the *Vanguard* for too long, Chet," she told him. "Besides, I'm needed at Edwards in ten hours."

"I'm a little worried, Leslie," he began. "I think Valentina might be replacing me next. She's sending someone from Baikonur."

"Not if our efforts with Lockhart worked," said Leslie. "He may come back to the Board for all we know."

"I hope so."

Hope: all that was left in these times. There was a silence sitting between the two of them. Leslie kept it going, trying to ignore Chet. It took some time for her friend to speak and break it.

"Well, goodbye."

This would be harder than she thought.

"I'll let you know what's going on when I get there," she informed him. "I've heard rumors the *Vanguard* is being weaponized. I really hope it's not being brought into any hostilities."

"I thought there were treaties against deployment of space based weapons."

Leslie sighed and said, "These are desperate times, Chet. Things get crazy in desperate times."

"Yeah."

"I'll be back."

"Yeah."

Leslie stopped packing.

"You don't believe me."

"Yeah."

"Chet, I'll be back."

"What if no one comes back anywhere? What if tomorrow the whole world goes to Hell for keeps? Look at what's been going on lately. There's no outright war yet, but the seeds have been planted. And that interview with McDaniel—."

"I'll be back, Chet."

"Yeah."

She never came back. After Leslie's departure, Chet was replaced, as predicted. He was transferred to a new project in Pearl Harbor involving the potential for exploration of water covered planets.

A Dark Sword would strike him down, and thereafter, he would join the drifting bodies.

BLITZ

The Dark Sword drone soared high above the snow covered mountains of northern China. The rhythmic rumble of its scramjet could only be heard from a few feet away, and due to its second generation nanopaint coating it made for the perfect stealth unit. Invisible to radar, heat *and* sound detection: genius.

As it neared its target the drone's railgun was readied via satellite command. The bullets, composed partly of depleted uranium, were loaded into the barrel of the gun. Soon, the attack would begin.

The line of armored communication vehicles was within range now. The drone's multi-lock targeting system allowed it to mark all of them with ease. It was time. The first shots would be fired off in fifteen...fourteen...thirteen...

The Dalai Lama was inside of an armored communication vehicle speaking with a member of Russian Internal Security. The wise one's smile was very broad.

"Yes, Your Holiness," the RIS member said. "It would seem that you have more than half of the country on your side now."

"I couldn't thank you more for what you are doing here," said the Dalai Lama. "It's always a pleasure working with you."

He had to leave now. He exited the vehicle and moved toward the transport he'd arrived in. He had only moved about a hundred feet when it happened. It was the most powerful sound he had ever heard in his entire life, maybe across multiple lifetimes. It was as if the Creator Itself had ripped the world in half and smashed the broken pieces together again. The old man was thrown to the ground by the subsequent shock wave, absolutely stunned by the noise. As he tried to recover, he touched a hand to his ear and looked at it. Blood was on the tips of his fingers.

The Dalai Lama looked back to find the vehicle he had just exited vaporized by the projectile that had been moving at four kilometers a second. He then realized what was happening and began running, not to the transport, but into the nearby forest. He knew this was an attack, and he knew that was merely the first round of the salvo. When he was much further away from the vehicles, he looked back. The piercing sound returned. He clasped his hands to his ears. Again and again it came, and again and again the vehicles were decimated by the blasts. Any that were only partially vaporized were hit again, and the job was finished. It was horrible. The men who had helped him were now being slaughtered, and he knew who had made this decision. He knew who had planned this attack.

Those operating his own transport had seen what was going on. They knew they wouldn't be able to back away quickly enough. They got out of the vehicle as fast as they could. Some weren't quick enough. The next shot hit and they were caught in the blast, vanishing into thin air instantly. The rest were knocked over, falling into the ground as the Dalai Lama had.

They didn't move. They hoped the firing would stop so long as they kept still. The Dalai Lama got low and did the same. All the vehicles in the area had been destroyed. There were no other major targets. After a few silent minutes, he realized it was over. He stood, and then the others stood.

"It's started," he whispered. But this wasn't where it started.

SIGNATURE

Brian McDaniel entered the briefing room swiftly, briefcase in hand. He sat at the table quietly and nodded to the others in the room. One of them was Daniel Lockhart, his smile saddened by recent incidents, but still carrying a spark of hope. The second of the three was the Deputy Director of the Defense Intelligence Agency, Morris Logan. He had a grim expression on his face, but Brian took no notice of it. The third man of the trio was a senior DIA briefer. He greeted Brian with a nod and introduced him to the others.

"We're glad you managed to make it, Mr. McDaniel," he said.

"I'm sorry I'm late," Brian told them. "I was busy reviewing the footage of my interview."

The grim expression weakened on the Deputy Director's face as he spoke, "If I do say so myself, I believe you did an impressive job, Mr. McDaniel."

"Thank you."

"Well," the briefer commenced, "now that you're here we can begin. Mr. McDaniel, the moment you informed Mr. Lockhart of the incident at the lab he had a conversation with the Deputy Director. Mr. Lockhart asked if he could have the DIA look into the break-in. We came across some very interesting findings."

"Such as?" Brian asked, hoping for a good answer.

"Well, for starters," the man went on, "we discovered that the security monitors and cameras had been disconnected for thirty-five minutes from 9:30 PM to 10:05 PM. The entire security team working at the lab claims to have seen no one enter or exit the facility during the time that the shutoff occurred."

"That was just after the interview ended, by the way," Daniel chimed in. Brian nodded to his friend and then said to the briefer, "Continue."

"We also found out something that indicates very substantial data. A special device was used to break through the touchpad lock on the door. We scanned it for an energy signature, and it turns out it was unlocked by a Chinese code cracker."

"Unbelievable," Brian said, shaking his head.

"Well, with the recent Dalai Lama incident," the Deputy Director told him, "it shouldn't be too hard to see something like this happening. I mean, you're whole goddamn statement was pretty much a 'screw you' to their religious suppression."

"True," Brian sighed. "My question is how they responded so quickly to the interview."

"The previews," Daniel spoke up. "There were previews airing about how you knew the cause of the madness in the days the leading up to the show. The Chinese could've seen any one of those."

"Yes," Brian said, now turning to Daniel, "but did any of those previews say anything about the intelligent design?"

"Who the hell knows?" Daniel replied. "Look, the energy signature says it all. This was a threat. Next time, it could be worse. We have to act."

"What's more," said the briefer, finally speaking up again, "the DIA has received reports that the Chinese may be mobilizing on the Federation's other half. Russia is in danger and we don't know why. We're not just going to wait until they hit us first."

"So you're going to use the break-in as an excuse for an act of war?" Brian began, surprised. "That's absurd! I'm one man and you're going to bank a whole war on me?"

Daniel seemed a bit on edge, too.

"I didn't mean for *this* to happen, Mr. Logan," he said. "I was hoping for some diplomatic action, but not war."

"They are mobilizing," the Deputy Director told them both. "This is our only opportunity."

"Daniel," Brian said, looking toward the man he spoke to, "this can't be happening. You know what this is. You know what's making these people aggressive."

He was right. Daniel looked to Morris Logan and said, "Mr. Logan, this man is correct. You need to reconsider this before—."

"The only reason," Morris interrupted, raising his voice, "we even offered to assist you when you asked, Mr. Lockhart, was because of how much you've contributed to the DIA. We didn't have to do a thing. Miss Valentina is the chairwoman of New Horizons now. You've stepped down. We don't need to heed your words any longer. The service of investigating the lab was complimentary. And now, after we've done so, you turn your back on us?"

"I didn't say—," Daniel began, only to be interrupted by Morris again, "This meeting is over. We're taking action now, whether you approve or not."

The cytologist was now the grim looking one. He should never have said anything. He had, though unintentionally, given rise to a war.

TRIGGER

The Supreme Chairman of Greater China sat before many people that day. To his left and right were his two top aides. Along both sides of the table were the chiefs of the three military branches. At the opposite end were three intelligence specialists. They had just finished presenting the evidence implicating the Russian half of the United Federation as a potential military threat. Intercepted electronic transmissions sent between Russian Internal Security and the Dalai Lama and satellite footage of him meeting with them recently were all that seemed needed to prove the Russians were working with the exile.

"So, Your Supremacy," the lead specialist began, in his own native language, of course, "what action do you plan to take now that you have this data before you?"

The Chairman's face was expressionless. He stared blankly across the table at the man who had spoken.

"I believe," he began, "that defeating the exile is not worth possibly losing our own people in vain. We will keep our guard up. If they attack, we will do what we must."

"There is one other thing, Your Supremacy," one of the specialists said. From under his seat he lifted a scrolled piece of paper. He stood up, walked over to the Supreme Chairman, carefully placed it down in front of the man, and watched as the leader of all Greater China lifted it and unrolled it. It was a poster, a poster depicting something that made fire glow in the man's eyes. Suddenly and swiftly, the Chairman ripped the poster in half.

"We will strike them with such *ferocity* that they will have no choice but to surrender the exile *immediately!*" he shouted, slamming a fist against the table. "This is no longer just a Chinese matter. *All* of Greater China is a part of this. Mobilize every available unit across all of our countries onto the Russian border. Send out the drones. This is a full-scale assault. They will pay for what they have done!"

The war had been ignited. The trigger had been pulled.

HYPE

The lonely man trudged through the sleet covered streets of Beijing. Rain and ice poured down on his shoulders, his head hanging low. He kept moving along, not knowing where he was going. He hoped he'd end up where he needed to be, wherever that was. He hoped that this wasn't all for nothing, that there was a good reason behind this. Hope was all he had, just as the multicast man had said.

Oh, but Kenro's career was over. He should never have been so rude in the presence of the Chairman. No one in the country would hire him. Word had spread. He was finished.

The slushy downpour grew stronger. Kenro could hardly see. He shut his eyes as a gust of wind rushed by. That's when he felt it. Something was pressing against his body, a thin obstruction. It was large, as though it were some sort of poster. He slowly pulled it off of his body and realized that there was something very interesting about it. He got on his knees and pressed it into the sidewalk. He then saw the image that would change everything.

The poster had upon it an illustration of the Dalai Lama. He wore a blue robe and was striding up the side of a mountain. At the mountain's peak, the sun shone brightly. At the mountain's base, darkness consumed all. In large, bold letters on the bottom of the poster a single word was imprinted: *FREEDOM.*

Kenro smiled and realized that all was not lost, that the end had not come yet. He once again recalled the Fox Global interview, and the cytologist. He couldn't locate the Dalai Lama, but he could possibly find *that* man. This was his only chance. War was coming, and he needed the cytologist's wisdom in this dark time. It was here he would make his move.

SPARK

The armored vehicle moved slowly through the snow covered forest. It left tread marks as it went along toward the first security checkpoint. When it stopped, the door on its right side opened and a man exited. He spoke with the guard on duty, then went back into the vehicle. The gates of the checkpoint slid open and they pressed on.

They were just outside the port city of Vladivostok, moving toward the regional headquarters of the RIS. Pressing matters were to be dealt with there. The head of the RIS, Grigory Yaroslav, was awaiting a special guest.

Checkpoint number two was passed through fairly quickly. This meeting would not be in vain, that was certain enough. Too much was at stake, and too close were these friends for one not to help the other.

The vehicle slowly pulled up to the third checkpoint. As the guard outside was spoken to, the passenger within remembered a time long ago when Grigory had assisted him in gaining the trust of the Chinese. It was to be done again. However, after the airing of the recent Brian McDaniel interview, it was apparent that this wouldn't be just a walk in the park.

They had now come to their final stop, and the passenger exited the transport. As he stepped out into the cold, he immediately started shivering.

"Right this way, Your Holiness," someone said as they approached him. He followed the speaker into the RIS Prime Compound. Once indoors, he sighed with relief. He, the Dalai

Lama, was then taken to Grigory's office. When he arrived he received a warm welcome.

"Jianyu!" Grigory cried as they hugged. "It has been too long!"

As they broke apart, the Dalai Lama smiled happily.

"Indeed," he began, "too long. How are you?"

"Great! And you?"

"I've seen brighter days," was the Dalai Lama's reply. Grigory's smiled faded a bit.

"Please, sit," he said. He motioned the others who had brought the Dalai Lama to leave the room, and asked one to bring the elder some tea. As they left, the door was shut. The two men sat and began their discussion.

"So, why have you requested me to bring my old body up here?" the Dalai Lama asked, to which Grigory replied, "Can two friends not talk every once in a while, just for fun?"

The Dalai Lama smiled again, "Please, Grigory, I know what this is about. You should not be worried about my being deported. It is merely a misunderstanding."

"Exile is not just a misunderstanding, Jianyu. Tell me, why did it happen?"

"I have said it once and I shall say it again: nothing happened. He just acted without reason. There was no thought of consequences, only malice."

As he spoke these words one of the men returned with the requested tea and handed it to the elder, who sipped from it carefully. The man then left quietly, bowing to the Dalai Lama and nodding to Grigory.

"My friend," the Russian began, "I understand that you do not wish for violent action to be taken. However, I must insist that you allow us to help you. We can assist you in communications with the people using, say, a large-scale propaganda campaign. Please, I am willing to offer any clandestine services you require from the RIS. It is my duty as your friend. I owe you more than my life for what you did for me."

The Dalai Lama's smile remained as he said, "You already helped me once. That meant a lot. You don't *have* to do anything this time."

"I'm aware of that."

In the Russian's book, refusal just wasn't on the table. Ultimately, the Dalai Lama was fine with this.

"Grigory, normally I would decline, but right now desperate measures are necessary. As long as no violence is used in restoring my influence, I am fine with it."

"It will be done, my friend. Let me show you back to your transport."

The Dalai Lama finished his tea, and as the two men exited the room someone was called over to take the teacup away from His Holiness. Soon, the elder was outside again. As he entered the armored vehicle, he looked back at Grigory. Both their eyes appeared to be reminiscent.

"I never asked how you survived that crash," said the Dalai Lama. Grigory laughed and answered, "Luck."

"There is no luck. You know that."

"Karma then."

The Tibetan's eyes glinted at the words. He had saved Grigory long ago after a transport crash. Though not truly a Buddhist, the Russian was one of his brightest and best pupils. He had challenged the wise one as a teacher, and as a friend. He even tested the elder's faith at one point, nearly causing him to lose sight of what he believed in, what he knew. But that was what made their bond so strong: the challenge, the test, the trial. It brought about a harmonious connection, a dance almost, one the Dalai Lama valued more than most things in this world.

"Karma then," said the teacher.

"Go on, Jianyu," said the student.

He did. He entered the vehicle, and the door was shut behind him by his friend. As the elder was sped away, he did not realize what had been going on while he had entered and exited the compound. A recording had been taken by an extremely powerful, cloaked satellite just then. This recording had footage of the Dalai Lama arriving at the compound and leaving it. The satellite was built in Harbin, Greater China. Not much else needs to be said.

BREACH

"The interview just ended. He should be back at the lab in exactly ninety minutes."

"We've got time."

"Don't get sloppy, Chekto. He wanted the operation to be done with precision."

"Don't worry, Roduk. I won't disappoint him."

The five operatives seemed to glide through the halls of the laboratory. They were each investigating one of the five levels of the building. The leader of the team, Chekto, was on the third level. He had to investigate each individual room of the level, thoroughly. He *had* to find the documents. If he didn't, his employer would be most displeased.

Upon arriving at each door, Chekto would ready his surface penetrating micro scanner. He would use this scanner to examine the room beyond. The operatives always needed to be one step ahead of anyone who may have been doing some late night work in the lab. At one point, Chekto came across a very interesting room. Rather than a doorknob, it had upon it a small numbered touchpad. The room was obviously bound by some sort of code. After using his micro scanner and finding no signs of life behind the door, Chekto readied his code cracker. He placed the flat piece of equipment on the touchpad, flipped the activation switch, and waited about six seconds. Then a sharp beep was emitted from the device and Chekto removed it from the pad. The door slowly opened before him, and he entered the room.

He knew this was his destination. Though it was a small room, he could feel the importance of it just by looking at it. Two desks were against either wall, each covered with open documents and files and the like. At the back of the room was an archive loader. Chekto knew that was where the data he needed was being kept. He then contacted the rest of his team.

"All eyes," he began, "on me; third level, room C13."

When the entire team had arrived, they began ripping the data from the loader. The physical documents on the desks were put into special cases while the digital documents were loaded into file cards. When the entire room was emptied of information vital to the mission, the team left quickly and quietly, making sure everything in the building looked as it did when they arrived (aside from what they had stolen, of course). As they exited the building, Chekto and Roduk spoke wirelessly once more.

"Is it done?" Roduk asked, to which the leader replied, "Indeed. McDaniel won't know what hit him."

"And you used the correct tools, right? The code cracker?"

"Yes, I did. Everything was done perfectly. You can reactivate the cameras now."

"Good work, Chekto."

The mission was complete. The team had done what they had needed to. Their employer would be very happy with their work.

ANSWER

"Klara has already explained the situation to me. She asked me to speak with you. I've already informed her of the change."

"Change, Mr. Lockhart?"

Daniel was speaking with Brian McDaniel. He was talking to the cytologist about the interview he'd requested on Multicast Worldwide, the New Horizons news multicast.

"I've been told," Daniel began, "by Klara about your evidence of the cause of the aggression."

"I see," said Brian, feeling somewhat relieved and yet somewhat worried. "And you needed to see me about that because?"

"I don't believe that Multicast Worldwide has the right audience for your announcement."

"Is that so?"

"Yes," Daniel went on. "I believe that an audience that would respond better to your data would be the Fox Global crowd. Though they're a competitor of ours, I have good relations with the Murdock family. They have a Sunday show that's extremely popular worldwide. It would make a much better approval test, if you don't mind me saying so."

"I don't mind at all, Mr. Lockhart," Brian told him, grinning. "As long as the information gets out there, I'll be just fine."

"I've already made the necessary calls. You've got your spot. Now, before you go, I have to ask you something."

"Yes?"

"Have you ever been interviewed on a live multicast before?"

Brian sighed and said, "Well, prerecorded definitely, but I actually haven't done any live work yet."

"Ah, well then, it's time to get a little practice in. I don't want you to bomb out there."

"Of course."

Daniel sat back and pulled from his coat a small paper.

"You came prepared for this?" Brian said. "I didn't know you cared."

"It's important this data gets out properly. I have my reasons. Let's take it from the top, just like broadcast prep. Just act as if the audience has already been told who you are and what you do."

After having said this, Daniel seemed to practically assume the identity of an interviewer. With both men at the ready, the practice run began.

"Good morning, Mr. McDaniel," the feign reporter said quickly, to which Brian replied, "Good morning, Mr. Lockhart. I'm honored to be on your show."

"*Glad.*"

"What?"

"*Glad*, not *honored*. Don't flatter them too much. Respect is good, but this is about you, not them. *You're* the reason people will be tuning in. *You're* the reason people are going to call their friends to switch multicasts."

"Right, right, I understand. Let me try that again."

"Whenever you're ready."

The cytologist sat for a moment, rapidly thinking over Daniel's advice. He then cleared his throat and said, "Good morning, Mr. Lockhart. I'm glad to be here today."

"Of course. Now, Mr. McDaniel, you claim to have promising evidence of what the cause of the mass aggression throughout the world may be. Please, enlighten us."

"Well, I'll..."

Sweat trickled down Brian's neck as he stared into the camera. Millions were watching him right now. He hoped not to disappoint Mr. Lockhart. That would be most unfortunate.

"I'll put it as simply as I can, Miss Evans," he began. "Do you remember when the CERN Collider science group began detecting evidence of intelligent design just before the program was shut down?"

"Of course," said the show's host, Brenda Evans. "The Origin Project: the one dealing with the super collider."

"That's the one," Brian continued. "The project procured some very interesting evidence, evidence of what is known as super symmetry. For those viewers who do not know, super symmetry is the idea that every particle in the physical universe has a 'super partner,' and that this 'super partner,' which initiates the existence of matter, consists of what is often referred to as pure energy."

"So what you're saying is this project discovered evidence of some sort of life force?"

"To an extent, Miss Evans," Brian went on, trying not to go on a tangent regarding her gross oversimplification of super symmetry. "Now, you know of the Caretaker Project, correct?"

"The one you're working on? Yes, I do. It's becoming mainstream knowledge slowly but surely."

"Well, I've been working on a side project. I started it upon the discovery of the Origin Project documents. I came by them via a good friend of mine who shall remain anonymous. This side project was essentially the very same thing as the Origin Project. I was extremely close to a breakthrough similar to theirs when, all at once, the basic nature of my research was *altered*. It was as if some sort of, for lack of a better term, *remote intelligence* had masked my discovery.

"When this occurred," continued the cytologist, "I looked back at the documents on the Origin Project. Apparently, similar circumstances had ended that project as well. There was inconsistency in the data of Origin near its completion, just like my own."

"So, you're saying that something intervened with your research?" Brenda asked, to which Brian replied, "For months, throughout my last stage of research, the energy signature remained consistent, just like the Origin Project. Then, about nine weeks ago, the energy signatures of all of my samples changed *simultaneously*, coincidentally on the same date the worldwide escalation of aggression began."

"And you believe this is all a result of some independent act by whatever it is that created the universe?" the host asked, and the cytologist answered, "To shed more light on the subject,

Miss Evans, I did another bit of testing just two days after the aggression began. I took advantage of my position on the Caretaker Project and examined the cellular patterns of several volunteer subjects' brains. They had *changed*."

"All of them, Mr. McDaniel?" Brenda asked.

"*All of them*, Miss Evans," Brian told her with utter certainty.

"Well, this is all very astonishing, Mr. McDaniel. But, I must ask, why would the very thing that created all that we know suddenly want to destroy it all?"

"I have a theory on that. Though it may sound unusual, it is possible that it is our own fault this has happened. For thousands of years, portions of humanity have believed that the world was to come to an end at one point or another. So far they've been wrong, but I believe that the number of people agreeing that the end is near has finally reached a high enough point that this remote intelligence is merely serving what's being asked for."

"Like how praying works in churches? This sounds a bit far-fetched. Your colleagues, no doubt, are at odds with this."

"True, Brenda. But, then again, this is an illogical situation we're dealing with here. There's only so much logic—that is, logic as *we* know it—that can be applied to it."

"Is it possible to counteract this, then?" Brenda asked the man. He replied, "How does one cut a diamond, Brenda? Once again, this is all theoretical. But, if we do not act soon, it will be too late. If too many people's patterns become altered, there will not be enough people to disagree with the madness. And when that happens, we are truly lost. I don't mean to drive your viewers into depression, but this is the cold hard truth and we need to fight it. It's now or never. Humanity's put all the chips in. All we have now is hope."

Brian McDaniel knew he was right. He just hoped everyone else did.

FATHER

"Mr. Lockhart, we've got to know what's going on."

"I already told you, I'm not talking about it."

Leslie had been trying to persuade Daniel to talk for a good fifteen, maybe even twenty minutes. Finally, Chet decided to speak up.

"Listen, Mr. Lockhart. We aren't asking much. In fact, I think we're actually offering quite a bit. If you tell us what happened to your son and why you stepped down, we may be able to help."

Daniel sighed. He couldn't hold it back. He knew that the only way to finish this was to face the truth. If he didn't tell the tale of his downward spiral, he would explode.

"This won't spread?" he asked. Leslie shook her head, telling him, "You have our word."

Chet nodded in agreement. Finally, Daniel spoke up.

"About two months ago," he began, "my son, Marcus, started acting a bit strangely. He kept telling my wife, Amy, when she put him to bed, that he had some weird ringing in his ears. She kept telling him every night that it would probably be gone in the morning. After the fourth day of the ringing, Marcus starting having tantrums. They were out of the blue. There was no real trigger for them or anything. He just got angry over any little thing. If Amy dropped a fork by accident, he'd yell at her for doing it. I'd send him up to his room and he'd stomp out of the dining area.

"It was when he killed his goldfish that I started getting really concerned," he continued, gesticulating at certain points during the tale. "He boiled the fishbowl. I still don't understand why he did it. That wasn't the worst of it though. While my wife was cooking one day, he..."

Daniel couldn't seem to bring himself to say it. He had his head in his hands. Then he felt a warm hand on his shoulder. He looked up to find Leslie's eyes very close to his own. They gleamed.

"We're here for you, Mr. Lockhart," she said softly. The man nodded slowly, and then he went on.

"I love my wife, you know. I love her so much. I just wish things could've happened differently. I wish I could've nipped this in the bud. She was dicing cucumbers when Marcus—I just don't get why—he ripped the knife out of her hand and cut her. I heard her scream from the bedroom. I'd arrived just in time, took the knife from my son, and kicked him away. He cried while I tended to Amy.

"We sent him to a therapist, but that didn't end well either. He lashed out at him too much and too harshly. Poor guy told us that Marcus couldn't be helped, that he was too dangerous. He recommended a well known hypnotherapist to do work on Marcus. I'm not a fan of hypnotism, so I told him I was fine without that being done. Amy suggested maybe if I started taking him for walks it would fix it. So, I did that. It worked for about a week, and then, just recently, he cracked again. I don't want to go into detail, but let me just put it this way: in defending myself, he was harmed more than expected. And now here I am, with my son. Amy's working now, but she should be here later."

Leslie's hand was still on Daniel's shoulder. Chet was smiling as his congratulations came forth, "See? Not so bad, huh?"

"I—I feel..."

Daniel couldn't speak. He just started weeping. It was sudden, but it didn't jar the other two. They got it. They really got it. That boy there wasn't just someone he'd hurt, it was someone he loved. He had done his best to keep that boy safe. He had failed *and* succeeded. Perhaps his failure outweighed his success. Perhaps it was the other way around. But he did love the boy, that was unmistakable.

My son. You're taking away my son. GIVE ME BACK MY SON!

His fist was clenched. He hadn't spoken, had he? Leslie and Chet were looking at him inquisitively. Was he happy, angry? What was that? He could hear—.

"Daniel?" Leslie interrupted his thoughts. Daniel's comlink was going off. He dried his eyes and reached into his pocket, pulling it out. He was surprised to find Klara's name on the caller ID. Upon pressing the acceptance button, he held the device to his ear.

"Klara?"

"Daniel, there's something we need to talk about."

SLAP

"These are all beautiful artifacts, Your Supremacy. But, when are you going to answer my question?"

Kenro was walking beside the Supreme Chairman of Greater China. Slowly pacing twenty-five feet behind them were two of the Chairman's top aides. They were within his personal museum, one building among many within the Supreme Compound. All throughout the halls were glass cases, and inside of these cases were antiquities spanning many centuries, such as weapons used in earlier eras or clothing worn by the ancient Chinese.

"Isn't it all so perfect?" the Chairman said, looking into one case containing an ancient set of armor. "An ancestor of mine wore this. Whenever I hear stories of him, I feel quite proud. His name, what was it...?"

"Your Supremacy," Kenro began, "I understand that this is all quite important to you. However, I need you to tell me why you've canceled Unification Day, as well as exiled the—."

"Don't speak his name in my presence. I have said it before, and I shall say it again: that man is a heathen monster. He has lied to me and my people. He deserved exile."

"When has he ever lied to us?" Kenro asked. The Chairman quickly spat, "Every word he has ever spoken to us is dishonest. He is a traitor and a fiend."

The two of them moved on to another artifact and, upon seeing it, Kenro's skin turned pale. No, he couldn't have done it. That was sacred!

"Ah, my prize," the Chairman began, "the Terracotta Warrior. I asked to have it brought to me upon becoming Supreme Chairman. Do you like it?"

"How did you have it taken from...?"

"I am the Supreme Chairman of Greater China. I can have whatever I ask for."

Kenro was infuriated. This man had canceled Unification Day, exiled the Dalai Lama, and taken an ancient Terracotta Warrior from the Chaanxi Province, not to mention his slaughter of innocents, which *still* hadn't desisted. It was pretty clear at that point who the heathen monster really was. The holographer's right hand clenched into a fist.

"Sir, all I came here for was a real answer to my question. You and the Dalai Lama were such good friends, and then out of the blue—."

"I told you *not to speak his name!*"

The museum, in all of its grandness, had fallen dead silent. The Chairman's aides had gone completely pale. Kenro was growing quite red, not with embarrassment, but with anger.

"Your Supremacy, with all due respect, have you gone completely out of your mind?"

One of the aides was gaping, while the other had pulled out his handkerchief and was rubbing his brow. The Chairman slowly turned to Kenro until their bodies were directly in front of each other. Then, in the blink of an eye, he raised a hand and slapped the award winning holographer across the face.

Kenro did his best not to react. His jaw tightened. His muscles were all tensed. His eyes widened and he began

98

breathing very heavily. Then, without a word, he walked away from the Chairman. He looked at the aides as he passed by them. Their legs were trembling, and one of them was swaying so much it seemed as if he would fall over at any moment. They were both gaping, one at the Chairman and the other at Kenro. Either way, it didn't matter.

As he left the museum, Kenro looked back down the hall toward the Chairman and cried, "Though I am ever loyal, sir, I am more than disappointed this day!"

His disappointment would only grow.

PROPOSITION

"For over sixty years, both the Chairman and I have been very good friends. I have respected him, and he has been equally responsive. Though recent events would drive a normal person into anger, my mind has not changed about the Chairman. He is still my friend, whether I am his or not."

The room was dark and quiet. Several men sat about a round table. They were within the Supreme Chairman's inner circle. The man speaking, in Chinese, of course, was the Dalai Lama. He spoke very slowly and very quietly, taking great care in what impression he left on the others.

"I am asking for your aid," he went on. "I ask for it in the same way a father asks for a son's aid. Though the bond may not be as strong, you all understand what I mean. I care dearly for the Chairman, but when things become desperate one must, at times, let go of things."

One of the men sitting down glared at the Dalai Lama.

"Are you asking us to betray our leader?" he asked, to which the Dalai Lama replied, "I am asking for helpers, not soldiers. I do not plan on overthrowing the Chairman. As I said before, he is my friend. I only wish to have you all bring him back to reality. He seems to have been recently possessed by some idea that I am a monster. I don't know where this idea has spawned from, but I do know that the source of the idea must be neutralized for a peaceful resolution to occur."

Another man across the table nervously asked the Dalai Lama, "You want us to eliminate a person who you believe is manipulating the Supreme Chairman?"

"Let me put it this way," the Dalai Lama began, slowly. "As you can tell, a large number of people have sided with me throughout the nation. Therefore, peace has been destabilized. If the 'manipulator' of the Chairman is taken care of, peace will stabilize. So, you can either help me, or you can be on the receiving end of a violent revolution."

One man stood up and said, "Are you threatening us?"

The Dalai Lama grew tense, hearing a slight ring in his ears, then said, "No, not at all. I merely meant to show you where your interest should lie."

The majority of the group seemed greatly offended, while a smaller portion seemed to be fine with the Dalai Lama's words.

"Though it may sound as if I mean to treat you as lesser men, I do not. All I can say is that this conflict needs to be addressed promptly and our only chance is to unite together, as we did once before on the day of the Rapprochement, the first Unification Day."

All was quiet for a moment. Something was throwing the Dalai Lama off. His skill in diplomacy was ordinarily far more refined than this. One member of the group spoke, "We are not betraying the Chairman. He is not being manipulated by anyone. This is his decision, and we must honor that."

"Is that what you believe?" the Dalai Lama asked, to which another member of the group replied, "I think that's what *we all* believe."

The Dalai Lama frowned. He then stood up and said, "Well then, it appears I am outnumbered. I do not wish to waste your time any longer. Good day to you all."

After that, he left and upon his departure, one man said, "You know what he'll do, don't you? He'll seek help."

"From whom?" someone asked. "It's not like he has anywhere else to turn."

DESPAIR

Daniel Lockhart sat beside the bed in which his son lay. When the doctor informed him that Marcus might not remember who he was when he woke, no tears were shed. Those waters had flowed already, freezing as they touched snow.

Daniel held the boy's cold, nearly lifeless hand in his own. He could feel the spark of energy still within his child. Knowing he had probably stolen Marcus' memories was bad, but at least he hadn't killed him. If that had happened, he'd have done more than just stepped down.

On the wall at the other end of the room was a viewscreen, on which Daniel noticed that the commercial break had finally ended and Multicast Worldwide was back on.

"Unmute," he said, and instantly sounds were released from the platform. The anchorman was just beginning his announcement about a very interesting subject.

"Welcome back, everyone. I'm Donald Stein, and you're watching Multicast Worldwide. Tonight, we have some startling news. We've been informed that the Supreme Chairman of Greater China has made an abrupt cancellation that's stirring up even more global trouble to go along with all the aggression already afoot. The annual holiday, Unification Day, which celebrates the multi-decade friendship between both the Dalai Lama of Tibet and the Supreme Chairman himself is being removed from the list of upcoming events on the Greater Chinese calendar, *permanently*. This has sparked a massive uproar throughout Greater China, and has evenly divided the nation's civilians into two parties.

"Dividing them even further," he went on, "was the announcement that the Dalai Lama will no longer be allowed within Greater Chinese borders. It has been declared by the Chairman himself that the Dalai Lama is, and I quote, '...a heathen monster who has lied to my people for a long time and for that reason deserves to be punished.' Immediately after the Chairman's announcement, massive riots erupted in both Shanghai and Hong Kong. The rioting in the former of the two is still going on currently. We'll now go live to our Shanghai correspondent, Cho Luan, for more."

The viewscreen cut to a short, thin Asian man standing in front of a terrifying sight. Daniel gaped. It was unbelievable. He'd only seen something like this once before, in a history class in grade school during his younger years.

"Thank you, Donald," said the man. He was speaking loudly in order to get his volume above that of his environment. "I am in the center of a massacre right now. Gunfire is unremitting and the screams of the horrified and injured are ceaseless. If you look behind me, you can plainly see that there is no end to individuals running in all directions. A full-scale military assault is being made on any and all protestors of the Supreme Chairman's actions, under *his orders*. I have received word from a source within the Chairman's inner circle confirming this as being the case. We are definitely in the middle of, dare I say it, a sort of holocaust."

Suddenly, a huge explosion could be seen in the upper right-hand corner of the viewscreen. Cho ducked, looked back, then turned to face the camera again, aghast.

"It appears that explosives are being used to knock out whole groups of anti-Chairman protestors simultaneously. As you can see, off in the distance, body parts are strewn about the street. It is a grisly sight, my friends. I..."

Cho appeared to be staring at something off in the distance. Then he gasped.

"Oh my God," he said. He then looked to the cameraman quickly and said, "We have to move. They're coming closer. Go, go, go!"

As both Cho and the cameraman began to run, it became hard to tell what was going on. However, it was quite obvious that both of them were in danger. As they pressed on, a few gunshots sounded and the cameraman stopped, dropping his equipment and giving the audience a sideways foot level camera view.

"Cho! Cho!"

Soon, Donald Stein was back on the screen, at which point Daniel Lockhart said, "Mute."

Too upsetting to handle was the conflict that was going on in the world. Daniel wished he could just shut it all out. But that would be cowardly. It wouldn't be right to avoid the conflict. He had to face it, and accept it, before he could do anything about it.

A knock came at the door. He stood up from his chair and, releasing his son's hand, approached and opened the door, revealing a nurse.

"Mr. Lockhart," she began, "there are two people here to see you. They say it's urgent and that they flew here from Washington."

"D.C. or state?"

"D.C., sir."

Daniel sighed, and then said, "Go ahead and send them in."

"Of course, sir," the nurse replied. With that, she was off.

BLOOMING

"Canceled? What? That's impossible!"

"I'm very sorry, s-sir. I know you p-put a lot of work into this event."

Kenro Chauren was appalled. He and his team had spent seven months preparing for Unification Day. The time and effort put into all of the lights and colors, the fireworks, the holographic theatrical performances and sculptures, the dance choreography, the parades, was all wasted now! How could this have happened? More importantly, *why* had it happened?

"I need to know more, Endru," he said to the bearer of bad news, and so the trembling man replied, "All that the Supreme Chairman has told me is that he is c-canceling the event and having His Holiness removed from the c-country."

"*He's* being exiled?" Kenro said, squinting in disbelief. "The *Dalai Lama* is being exiled? How can the leader of the entire nation be so disgraceful? I have never heard of a more—GAH! Why would he do that?!"

"I d-don't know. You could always ask him yourself. You'll be more than welcome th-there, considering your high p-prestige."

"I think I'll do exactly that."

"I sh-shall inform him of your coming arrival."

Endru seemed as if he were about to faint.

"Don't worry, Endru," Kenro told him. "It isn't your fault. You're just a representative. Let the Chairman know I'll be meeting him very shortly. I have to deliver this news to the rest of my team."

"Of course, sir," Endru said, sounding a little more relieved. "Thank you."

"Don't mention it," Kenro told him. "Oh, and one more thing?"

"Yes, sir?"

"How's your brother doing? I haven't heard from him since..."

"He's," Endru began slowly, "all right. It was his own fault. I still don't know why he attacked that man. It was strange, irrational."

"I see," Kenro replied. "Very well. You may go."

"A good day to you, sir."

"And to you."

Endru left. Kenro was alone now, just outside the Beijing Concert Hall. Well, not alone. More than thirty million lived in this city. As they passed, those who recognized him waved and beamed. He forced a smile and waved back. He took note of their faces, the smiles, the care, the love. He didn't know it yet, but such expressions would be rare in the coming days. They would be replaced by clenched fists and furrowed brows, fiery eyes and gritted teeth, shouting, screaming, bleeding, breaking, volcanic eruptions, ash.

Was it inevitable? Kenro didn't know. He hadn't even been slapped yet. He hadn't seen the interview. He hadn't found the poster. He hadn't gone to America to find Brian. He hadn't gone with him to see Daniel. He hadn't gone to L.A. with them to witness the world's destruction. He hadn't grown angry, like the Chairman, like Endru's brother, like the Presidents with their scalar weapons and their particle beams. None of that had happened yet.

Kenro didn't know.

He had pulled a chip out of his pocket. It was active, projecting a holographic flower he had crafted for an important day. It wasn't any kind that had ever grown on Earth. It was his own creation. It had twenty-one petals, appearing in three layers: ten on the bottom, seven in the middle, four on the top. The stem and sepals were a deep purple, while the petals and stamen were bright pink, changing to aquamarine and scarlet red at timed intervals. It could be expanded in size so as to be used for a parade float. It was never used.

"Pretty!"

A little girl was passing by with her mother, reaching for the flower. Kenro didn't need it anymore. The mother tried to pull her daughter away, but the holographer handed the chip to the girl, hologram still active. The little one giggled, and the mother thanked Kenro. He nodded, and turned away to enter the Hall.

Was this inevitable?

DISCOVERY

"Miss Valentina, there is someone here to see you. He's been checked out."

"Send him in."

Klara Valentina sat alone in her temporary office. From behind her desk she watched as her guest entered the room. He was short, a bit potbellied, and balding. He wore a gray suit and a ruby red tie in contrast with it. In his right hand he held a briefcase.

"Please, sit," Klara said as the door was closed behind the man. He sat in the chair just in front of her desk and extended a hand in greeting.

"It is a pleasure to meet you, Miss Valentina," he began as she shook his hand. "May I take the time to congratulate you on your recent nomination?"

"Of course," said Klara, looking the man over thoroughly. "I've been receiving such praise quite frequently. It's enjoyable, knowing you're part of something big. But enough of that. Who are you and what brings you to my office?"

"My name is Brian McDaniel," said the man. "I'm a—."

"Clinical cytologist," Klara finished off. "Yes, I've heard of your work on the Caretaker Project. Nerve cell duplication; the ability to replace nerve pathways. Very nice."

"Thank you, ma'am," Brian said, smiling. "It's good to know someone takes note of my work. Anyhow, I was wondering if you could do me a favor."

"And what might that be?"

"I need to get an interview spot on the New Horizons multicast. The people of the United Federation must hear of my discovery."

"Is that so?"

"Yes," Brian went on, "it is."

"What exactly is it that you've discovered, Mr. McDaniel?" she asked, her eyes thinning. Brian plopped his briefcase onto the desk and opened it up. He then reached in and pulled out a folder. After closing the briefcase and removing it from the desk, Brian opened the folder and set it in front of Klara.

"I'm sure you've heard of or noticed the recent outbursts," said Brian, to which Klara replied, "Indeed. They're becoming more and more frequent by the day."

After looking over the folder's contents for a few minutes, Klara looked up at the cytologist. Her eyes were stern.

"You are claiming that this is the cause of the fighting?" she said to him, at which point Brian answered, "Every indicator points to that being the case. Not only that, but I have a significant amount of evidence to back it up which any independent group of cytologists can examine. This is *very* promising."

"And you believe that the average civilian will agree with this?"

"I'm not certain as of yet, but the multicast announcement will make for a good test of approval. This data must be made known. Please, I'm begging you. All I need is fifteen minutes."

Klara remained silent for a moment. She then closed the folder and pushed it across the desk.

"I will give you a ten minute spot on the platform. But before you go, I must ask why you came to me about this rather than those working at Multicast Worldwide. I don't see why it was necessary to speak with me, the chairwoman, about such a matter."

"It's a long story, Miss Valentina," Brian told her. "Let's just say I had to take a more drastic approach after being denied."

Klara grinned.

"I see," she said. "All right. You may leave now."

"Thank you, Miss Valentina."

With that, Brian McDaniel took his folder and briefcase and exited the office of Klara Valentina.

RESIGNATION

Colonel Leslie Thompson walked slowly off the departure ramp. She had just taken a shuttle down to Earth from her station aboard the *Vangaurd*, a ship owned by Starbound Enterprises. She smiled as she spotted her good friend, Chet Glenhood. The smile faded when she noticed his frantic expression.

"Leslie!" he called out to her from across the docking bay.

"Chet, what's wrong?" she asked when they were closer together. "You look like you've seen a ghost."

"Leslie, something crazy just happened," Chet began. "Daniel Lockhart just stepped down as Chairman of New Horizons."

"From the Board?"

"Yes," said Chet. "He says he's too emotionally compromised to hold his post and that he needs to leave the company."

"Has a replacement been selected yet?" Leslie asked him, to which he replied, "That's what has me worried. He said he's having a friend of his, some politician from the Federation's other half, fly in to be a temporary fill-in while the choice is being made. And get this: she's the same one who Mikhail Gavrikov appointed as his vice presidential nominee."

"Klara Valentina? I thought she was busy getting ready for the Russian election."

"She is," Chet told her. "She's doing this at Daniel's request. Apparently she's known for being good at multitasking or something."

"Well, why does it matter?" said Leslie. "Everything's fine here, right? No trouble?"

Chet sighed and said, "Valentina is letting a lot of American folks go. She wants more of 'her kind' working here."

"You've got to be kidding me!" Leslie exclaimed. Chet shook his head and said, "I know. It looks like my job may be next. Every company under New Horizons is being affected in the same way."

"What could've caused Lockhart to become emotionally compromised?"

"I wish I knew," Chet said gloomily.

"Well," Leslie said, looking back at her shuttle as it departed, "we had better find out and see if we can fix it. You know how we can contact him?"

"He lives up in Vermont. I think he's receiving a lot of attention right now. You really think he'll let us see him?"

"You're the overseer of the entire Shipwright Division down here, and I'm a high ranking officer up on the *Vangaurd*. Chet, this is his baby. He'll see us."

"I hope you're right."

"I'm right."

GIFT

A cool breeze pressed against Daniel Lockhart's face. Snow had fallen in Vermont and so he decided to take his little boy, Marcus, out for a walk. The child was dancing about happily, stopping every once in a while to plop down on the ground and make a snow angel. He wanted to "leave his mark." As they moved along, Daniel couldn't help but chuckle a bit at Marcus. It was adorable the way he pranced about, pointing out the littlest things to his father as if he'd made some new discovery.

The boy's thoughts had been disrupted by something, a thing unknown, a thing unseen. It made his ears ring and ignited an abnormal rage within the child. Whatever it was, it wasn't affecting him now, and that was all that mattered. Nothing made Daniel happier than seeing Marcus free of the anger, free of the upset. Here, he wouldn't hurt anyone, and here he wouldn't be hurt. Here, he could breath and be alive, sane, honest, fun.

Here, he could play.

After some time, Daniel decided to show Marcus how to make a snowball. The child quickly caught on to the concept of throwing them at people and the two got into a battle.

"Bow before me, rebel scum!" the father shouted, tossing one. "I am—uh—Trellgore, King of the Ninth Galaxy!"

Marcus laughed and fired back. He was good at dodging, almost as good as his father. Against a lesser opponent, he might have proven to be a good shot, too. But this was Daniel Lockhart he was facing, a champion of snowball warfare.

Hitting him would be about as easy as—oh! There it was! Daniel laughed, and Marcus laughed, and it was such fun!

Something was odd though. As they kept playing, Marcus kept throwing the snowballs harder and harder, as if actually trying to cause pain with them. When another one had hit Daniel, it felt like ice had been packed inside. Then, after a while, Marcus' face grew less happy and seemed more intense, even angry. He stopped throwing the snowballs.

"Hey, buddy," Daniel called over to him, "you okay? Did I hit you too hard?"

Marcus' jaw stiffened, and then he grew wild and ravenous. He bared his teeth and panted heavily, clenching a fist.

"Marcus?" Daniel said, now very worried about his son. It was happening again. He approached him with caution, but before he could come too close the boy leaped at him. He grabbed onto his father's neck tightly and pressed his thumbs deep into his father's windpipe. As he did so, Daniel tried to find some alternative to fighting back, some way of saving himself without causing harm to his child.

There was none.

They wrestled around, and Daniel fell over on top of the boy. He pulled his son away from him and began to shout at him. Tears stung the father's eyes. *Please control it, Marcus!* The boy punched his own father in the face. Daniel stood up, away from Marcus. No, no, no, not like this. Again the child charged him and leaped upon him. Daniel then, with all the force he could muster, grabbed the boy, the boy he loved, and threw him aside.

A crack could be heard.

116

"MARCUS!"

Daniel was sobbing over the body of his son. His head had crashed into a rock. His skull was fractured. Blood oozed from it into the snow. He had killed him. The child was dead.

Wait, a heartbeat? No, it had to be a hallucination, a trick of the mind, it wasn't real. But it was! It had to be! Marcus was breathing, if only just. Emergency services were contacted. Blood was repressed by the clothes of the father. The boy would live.

Was it really a collapse? Was what happened really an end to humanity? What if it wasn't? What if, in truth, this was salvation in the guise of destruction, life appearing as death, harmony seeming to be chaos, an end that was really a beginning? The outcome seemed worth the price: an ideal Man, living on their Eden, free of Evil, full of Good. Even if that wasn't the intent, it was the result: an everlasting utopia.

That being said, what *was* the intent?

BEACON

The Instrument was traveling at thirty parsecs a second. It had passed through several galaxies during its speedy journey and was finally decelerating. As it slowed down, it drew ever closer to its target. It was the third planet orbiting the star of this system. Multiple continents carrying billions of inhabitants, all unaware of their impending demise. Closer drew their silent killer, the tiny device that would soon silence them *permanently*.

The Instrument was now just a few thousand miles from the planet's atmosphere, and within a quarter of a second it was about one hundred and sixty miles above its surface in near polar orbit. After stabilizing itself, the Instrument began to emit a very sharp, precise beeping noise repeatedly. The rhythmic pulse of the hypnotic had begun. Soon it would seep into the minds of all of the planet's inhabitants. They had no means of resistance.

And so their ears would ring. And so their fists would clench. And so their time had come.

VERDICT

And here is where all begins and ends.

Krylus' fingers clicked across the metal table. His yellow eyes glowed dimly. He knew this meeting's end was nigh. The one called Darsuul was speaking.

"Have you been observing them lately? They are animals! Therefore, they should be slaughtered like animals!"

The other thaddeons had been debating back and forth for quite some time. It wouldn't be long before these machine bodied beings made their decision.

"If they are to be killed, it cannot be done in such an obvious fashion, Darsuul," one member responded. "Their memories may carry on into their next lives. We will be discovered."

Although most of the Council was for the execution of the operation, there were some who would not allow such an action to be taken on the humans.

"They should be given a chance," spoke the only female member. "They do not deserve this. Who cares if they are ambitious?"

"First of all, it is not their ambition that has caused them to be put in this position," Darsuul began. "It is their arrogance, their intolerance and their violence that have made them a target. They are a threat and must be neutralized. And secondly, they *have* been given chances, far too many at that. It is time we gave them what they deserve: their doom."

"Is that so?" the female retorted, pulling her head back in anger. "Well, after having witnessed their reboot personally, I completely and utterly disagree with you, Darsuul. They have evolved intellectually, technologically and spiritually in ways we have not seen before. And furthermore, I believe that your decision is based on fear and fear alone. You fear the competition the humans will provide, their diverse nature, and you fear that they may become intelligent enough and powerful enough to overpower us."

"Is that such a bad reason?" Darsuul inquired rhetorically. "They are too dangerous. They must be taken care of now, before they grow into a greater power. What if they discover we rebooted them? What if they seek revenge? Are you willing to be responsible for the destruction of the entire thaddeon race?"

Krylus was now done waiting for a more unanimous decision. He was ready to end this.

"That is enough," he said firmly. His eyes scanned over each of the members of the Council, one by one. He then said, "It is time we took a vote. I will call each of you by name, and you shall say 'aye' or 'nay.' The majority vote will be victorious."

Krylus quickly looked to each Council member and spoke their name very crisply, and each replied quickly and without hesitation. Soon enough everyone had voted, and a perfect tie was drawn.

"Well," Krylus started off, straightening his posture, "I see that I am the swing vote here. The fate of their world rides on my shoulders."

The room was dead silent. You could hear a feather touch the floor it was so quiet. No one dared move, save Krylus.

"My brother," he began, breaking the silence, "left not long after the human reboot. Does anyone here know why?"

No one answered. No one knew.

"He called the reboot a mistake. He called *every* reboot a mistake. He called the Council a mistake, our galactic regulation a mistake, our reasons for doing so mistakes. It was all wrong to him, just an endless series of mistakes, lies and conspiracies."

Why was he saying this?

"He didn't say those things because he was angry, or confused, or deranged. He said those things because he was honest. If he felt a certain way about something, he told you. He *always* told you. He didn't care if you didn't like it; if it was the truth, he let you know."

Darsuul and the female exchanged looks, then turned back to Krylus.

"I have made great efforts, since his egress, to be as honest as my brother was. And so, though many of you will clash with my choice, it is, at the very least, the truth. And, in the end, that is all that has ever mattered, and all that *will* ever matter."

They all knew what he meant.

"I have made my decision," he said, "and that decision is..."

Dylan Alexander,

13 when he first began publishing his books, began writing stories at the age of 6. This is one of his first published works of many more exciting stories to come.

For more information on the author and to read and learn about more of his stories and upcoming works, please visit www.WyndryderPublishing.com.

www.ingramcontent.com/pod-product-compliance
Lightning Source LLC
Chambersburg PA
CBHW060639130626
46555CB00002B/870